The Affair of the Empress's Little Finger

(annotated)

By G. H. Teed

Illustrated by Valda and Parker

Edited by Doug Frizzle

First Published in the Union Jack magazine, No. 1121, 4 April 1925.

Stillwoods Edition

Stillwoods.Blogspot.Ca

Catalogue Information:
Title: The Affair of the Empress's Little Finger (annotated)
Author: G. H. Teed (1886-1938)
Illustrated by: Eric Parker (cover) and J. H. Valda (interior)
Edited by: Doug Frizzle (1949-)
First published anonymously in the Union Jack magazine, No. 1121, 4
     April 1925.
This Edition by: Stillwoods, 2024
ISBN Canada: 978-1-998819-37-9
Blog: Stillwoods.Blogspot.Ca
Author Blog: http://ghteed.blogspot.com/
Old Storefront: http://www.lulu.com/spotlight/lulubook22

https://tinyurl.com/ve25d42s This link should go to a spreadsheet of all known Teed stories. The list is annotated with various information on the stories and my progress with recapturing the work. The library of Teed's stories increases almost weekly. Check at Amazon and Lulu.Com for the earlier publications. Search for (space)Teed. /drf

Keywords: Sexton Blake, Tinker, Hong-Lo-Soo, London

Cautionary Note: This series of books by Stillwoods are intended to make the stories of G. H. Teed, born in New Brunswick, Canada, available to collectors and researchers. The editor, or rather digitizer has not altered the original publication.

This story may contain language and racial terms that are not appropriate today. I apologize for them; I know that the author was using his voice to excite and entertain an adventurous English audience. These works were published from 82 to 110 years ago. Most every work has characters of redeeming ethnicity within.

I hope you enjoy and share these stories; I have.

Doug Frizzle

Contains racial terminology which is inappropriate today.

Featuring Hsui-Fsi and Hong-Lo-Soo.

Contains racial terminology which is inappropriate today.

SEXTON BLAKE in a weird detective mystery —
COMPLETE IN THIS ISSUE.

> You will begin to ask yourself questions before you are through the first two chapters of this gripping yarn. What was the mystery of the cottage in Devonshire? Why the Chinese atmosphere about the place? What was the curious Eastern odour? And what the voices in the night? Sexton Blake asked himself these same questions, too — and a very curious explanation he found! When you have started this yarn you won't need to worry what to do with the next hour or two of your time.

Introduction to the Annotated Edition

- Facsimile Reproduction
- Supplementary Information
- Historical Context
- Collectors' Commentary
- Author Biographical Notes
- Guide and listing of 'Independent' stories

This Stillwoods collection is about the author G. H. Teed. The great majority of his 500+ stories were written anonymously. They also, at the time, were issued under copyright —under the Sexton Blake banner. Teed wrote from 1913 until his death at the end of 1938. Since most of these works were anonymous, no-one knew he was a Canadian —or at least I have never seen a mention.

Teed's novels appeared in 'pulps' mostly —magazines with cheap paper, and issued mostly on a weekly basis. In original format, they are difficult to obtain today in undamaged condition. And they can be expensive!

Included in the ancillary material is the usual advertising for the next weekly issue.

Digitized by Doug Frizzle. This story may have also been digitized by others. Often those copies revise offensive terminology; I have retained the original terms only to indicate acceptable language of the day. Again I apologize to anyone that might be offended.

Seldom did any of Teed's Sexton Blake stories not feature one of Teed's famous and recurring villains. George Marsden Plummer, Dr. Huxton Rymer, and Wu Ling are perhaps the best known.

This novel has no familiar villain. But it is a great little story, and after reading it, I am asking myself—since there are only a handful of them —perhaps I should next digitize this remaining handful. This one is very entertaining and interesting.

While the title page has the spelling 'Empress's', the cover page of the original was 'The Affair of the Empress' Little Finger'. I have altered the cover for consistency.

/drf

The SB works of G H Teed in the "Union Jack" and "The Sexton Blake Library" **without** the usual villain. This list is, for me, of particular interest because they are works outside of the usual formula.../drf

From a Collectors' Digest file at 'friardale.co.uk', dated about 1952.

With some Notes on certain characters created by him, the List by Bill Colcombe, checked by Len Packman and Harry Homer; the Notes by Bill Colcombe and Harry Homer.

G. H. TEED'S work in "THE UNION JACK"

iv

The Affair of the EMPRESS's LITTLE FINGER

Pictures by
J H VALDA

You will begin to ask yourself questions before you are through the first two chapters of this gripping yarn. What was the mystery of the cottage in Devonshire? Why the Chinese atmosphere about the place? What was the curious Eastern odour? And what the voices in the night? Sexton Blake asked himself these same questions, too—and a very curious explanation he found! When you have started this yarn you won't need to worry what to do with the next hour or two of your time.

THE FIRST CHAPTER.

A Collision, a Captain, and a Chink.

IT certainly was not Tinker's fault. Even the victim, when he recovered consciousness, acknowledged that. Tinker was on his right side of the road, and not doing more than twenty when the motor-cyclist came flying round a curve—a blind curve concealed by high hedgerows—and dashed head-on into the Grey Panther.

The front wheel of the motor-cycle hit the "bumper" of the car just as Tinker jammed on the brakes. It was the steel bumper that Blake had had put on a month or so before that probably saved the life of the cyclist and Blake and Tinker from serious injury from a smashed wind-shield.

The impact was terrific, and the force of it hurled the cyclist from the saddle into the air. He described a parabola before thudding to the ground on the other side of the hedge. The motor-cycle leapt clean over the car and crashed to the road beyond, where it somersaulted half a dozen times or more before ending up in a tangle of wreckage against the stone wall at the base of the hedgerow.

Blake and Tinker had a marvellous escape. The Grey Panther, thanks to the heavy steel bumper, stood the shock well, although, in its leap into the air, the motor-cycle gave the right wing a nasty twist and carried one of the road lamps clean off.

Tinker was over the side almost before the car had come to a stop. He scrambled up the side of the bank and managed to get over the hedge. In the grass on the other side he saw the huddled body of the cyclist, quite unconscious, and with a stream of blood oozing down from under his hair.

Tinker ran across and bent over him. He got his arms under the young fellow's shoulders and straightened him out; then he dropped to his knees to try and discover the extent of his injuries. He soon found the wound in the top of the scalp from which the blood was coming, and he pursed his lips anxiously

THE FIRST CHAPTER.

A Collision, a Captain, and a Chink.

IT certainly was not Tinker's fault. Even the victim, when he recovered consciousness, acknowledged that. Tinker was on his right side of the road, and not doing more than twenty when the motor-cyclist came flying round a curve —a blind curve concealed by high hedgerows —and dashed head-on into the Grey Panther.

The front wheel of the motor-cycle hit the "bumper" of the car just as Tinker jammed on the brakes. It was the steel bumper that Blake had had put on a month or so before that probably saved the life of the cyclist, and Blake and Tinker from serious injury from a smashed wind-shield.

The impact was terrific, and the force of it hurled the cyclist from the saddle into the air. He described a parabola before thudding to the ground on the other side of the hedge. The motor-cycle leapt clean over the car and crashed to the road beyond, where it somersaulted half a dozen times or more before ending up in a tangle of wreckage against the stone wall at the base of the hedgerow.

Blake and Tinker had a marvellous escape. The Grey Panther, thanks to the heavy steel bumper, stood the shock well, although, in its leap into the air, the motor-cycle gave the right wing a nasty twist and carried one of the road lamps clean off.

Tinker was over the side almost before the car had come to a stop. He scrambled up the side of the bank and managed to get over the hedge. In the grass on the other side he saw the huddled body of the cyclist, quite unconscious, and with a stream of blood oozing down from under his hair.

Tinker ran across and bent over him. He got his arms under the young fellow's shoulders and straightened him out; then he dropped to his knees to try and discover the extent of his injuries. He soon found the wound in the top of the scalp from which the blood was coming, and he pursed his lips anxiously as he saw that it was a long, nasty-looking gash. He ran his hands over the shoulders, arms, body, and legs of the other, but could not seem to find any broken bones, although he could not tell how bad his internal injuries might be.

Then he pressed his ear to the unconscious one's heart and

listened.

It was beating jerkily, but with apparent strength, and at this he got to his feet and ran back to the hedge. Blake was standing in the road preparing to climb up if necessary.

"He has had a nasty knock on the head, guv'nor," the lad announced. "It is a bad cut, and it's bleeding freely. I can't find any broken bones, but he is unconscious, so I don't know for sure yet. Will you throw up your flask from the pocket inside the door, and I will see if I can bring him round."

"I'll bring it up," said Blake.

He turned back to the car and took out a leather-covered flask from under the flap of the front door. Then he scrambled up the bank and crawled over the hedge. He went across and knelt down beside the limp figure of the young fellow who, through his own recklessness, had brought himself to such a pass. Blake's examination followed just about the lines which Tinker's had taken, and then he took out his handkerchief and wiped away the worst of the blood from the wound.

"Hold his head!" he ordered. "That's it! Let us see if we can get some of this brandy down his throat."

He forced some of the spirit between the young fellow's lips, and stroked the throat to help it down. But it only trickled out of the corners of the mouth, and Blake shook his head. He raised himself and looked about. About half a mile away across the fields he saw a group of buildings, and nodded towards them.

"There is a farm," he said. "We shall have to try and get him there, and then we must find a doctor. He has had a bad crack on the head —may be concussion. Give me a hand, Tinker, and we will get him down to the car."

Between them they managed to get the limp body over the hedge and slide it to the road, where Tinker supported it until Blake joined him. Then they lifted it into the tonneau and Blake sat beside it, his arms supporting it, while Tinker again took the wheel.

He drove slowly along until they came to a pair of gates on the left side of the road, and here he paused to jump down and open them. Then he drove through, and after closing the gates drove on towards the house which was set among the group of farm buildings which they had been able to see across the fields.

It was early afternoon of a spring day, and Blake and Tinker had

2

been motoring up to London from Devonshire, where Blake had been on a case which had proved to be a matter of routine, and which Tinker could have handled perfectly well unaided. They had lunched at Exeter and were trundling along at a good pace, intending to make town before dark if possible, when the accident had occurred.

They could not, of course, leave the young fellow back in the field, no matter how much at fault he may have been. Neither Blake nor Tinker was that sort of motorist.

At first there did not seem to be anyone about the place into which they had driven, but when Blake had hallooed several times the back door of the house opened and an elderly man with a wooden leg hobbled out. He stood looking at them for a few moments, then he came across to where the Grey Panther was standing.

"I am sorry to intrude upon you." Blake said courteously, "but there has been an accident. This young fellow charged us with his motor-cycle, and he seems to be rather badly injured. Will you permit us to bring him inside, and perhaps you can tell us if we can get a doctor near here?"

The one-legged man, who had appeared to have a tumour inside his left cheek, turned his head a trifle and spat out tobacco-juice. Then he nodded.

"Bring him in if you want to," he said. "But I'll tell you now that he got no more than he deserved. These dang autymobillies and sechlike be the pest of the countryside. Shiver my wooden leg, but I'd have the whole dang lot scrapped if I had my way."

Blake smiled inwardly. At very first sight of the farmer he had thought:

"Looks more like an old sea-faring man than a farmer, and one who has sailed the Seven Seas at that." And now, from the words the other had uttered, he knew that his first impression had been correct. Then his eyes twinkled.

"You may be right, captain," he said in a casual tone. "After all, there is nothing like a good deck under one's feet and a full spread of sail. But modern times, modern means, you know."

The other looked at him agape.

"I don't think I know you," he said at last. "Where have I met you?"

"Never before to my knowledge," answered Blake, with a smile, as he opened the door and started to help Tinker lift the unconscious

3

fellow out of the car.

"Then how did you know I was a sea captain?"

"The air of the whole Seven Seas hangs over you," said Blake. "Nothing will ever wipe out that stamp, captain. Am I right?"

"Dang it all, but you be. I sailed the Seven Seas for forty year and more."

"And, like nearly every other sailor, you always pined for a farm ashore," finished Blake.

The old man nodded and lent a hand with the burden. He gave Blake more than one curious glance as they went along to the house, for he was considerably startled at the ease with which this stranger had placed him in his niche in life, even down to the hopes he had carried inside his heart for all those years when he had been scraping about foreign ports. But he said nothing more then, for all their care was needed with the injured man.

They entered a small but very comfortable and spotlessly clean kitchen, and then on into a sitting-room which had more the appearance of a ship-shape cabin at sea than a room ashore. If Blake had needed any further proof of what he had ventured he had it there.

At one side of the room was a sort of bunk couch, above which hung a telltale compass, and Blake shrewdly guessed that it was here the old mariner had been taking his ease when he had heard his hail. On a black teak table at one side were some marine books, a dingy-looking cutty pipe, a wad of black-jack, some odd-looking shells, and other bits of junk.

On every side were evidences of the previous roaming of the old man, from the giant polished turtle-shell, which had been fixed against one wall, and the medley of strange weapons which had been stuck in every conceivable place, to the bits of gear which hung here and there, just as if the captain had but come down from his spell on deck. It was just as near his own sea-cabin as he could make it, and that was easy to see.

They laid the unconscious man on the bunk, and then, in response to Blake's repetition of the question, the captain informed him that a doctor lived just on the outskirts of the village, some five miles away. Blake got his name and then sent Tinker off in the Grey' Panther to fetch him. In the meantime he and the old mariner set to work to try and bring the young fellow round, and at the end of ten minutes they succeeded.

Blake was relieved to find that his mind cleared gradually, and knew from this that if the skull had been injured it could not be as bad as had looked at first.

They bathed the wound in hot water and gave him some spirit, and then kept him quiet until they heard the sound of footsteps outside the door. A moment later Tinker entered, accompanied by the doctor, a kindly-faced, middle-aged man, typical of the hardworking medicos who give up their lives to a career of what is almost oblivion in the depths of the country.

Blake introduced himself, and a light of recognition came into the medico's eyes. Blake had not told his name to the captain, and that worthy now began to hammer the point of his wooden leg on the floor in excitement.

"Dang my old timbers! I knew you must be out of the ordinary to spot me like you did," he said. "Sexton Blake! Hey! I've heerd a lot about you. You hev been out on the Chiny Coast a good deal. I've heerd of you there. Be you the same?"

Blake smilingly confessed that he must be, and from that moment the old mariner seemed to lose all interest in the unfortunate young fellow who had tried to ram the Grey Panther.

And as the accident has little or nothing to do with the events which followed that visit of Blake's to the farm of the retired sea captain, it may be as well to state briefly that, after a prolonged examination, the doctor stated that the victim would be all right, that no bones were broken, and that he could find no signs of internal injuries. It seemed that the wound on the head and the shock of his fall was all that was the matter with him, but he did advise strongly that he should remain at the farm overnight in order to see if any complications arose.

Blake agreed with this, and since it was plain now that they could not make London until late, he agreed readily with the next suggestion, that he should also stay at the farm and bring the young fellow along in his car the next morning, so that the doctor could have another look at him as they passed through the village. The old mariner seemed eager that Blake and Tinker should fall in with this, so they fixed it that way.

Shortly after Tinker drove the doctor back home, and when they were gone Blake turned to his old host.

"I hope you will be able to manage with three unexpected guests, captain," he said; as he drew out his cigar-case and held it out. "My young assistant and I can give you a hand if necessary."

"Dang me, no, Mr. Blake," came the explosive answer. "I'm all shipshape here, with a good galley and a good cook. Don't you worry about that."

And before Blake had time to reply a liquid voice sounded behind him.

"Me velly good cook. Me fixee all light. All be one piece top sidee. You see!"

Blake swung round like a shot, and there, in the shadow by the polished turtle-shell was a Chinaman, smiling blandly, as if he had been there all the time.

Nor could Blake be sure now that he hadn't, for he had been standing facing the door, and he was hanged if he could figure out how the Celestial could have come in without him seeing him. And if he hadn't come in by that door, then how had he entered? As far as Blake could see, that was the only door.

Had the yellow man been there all the time?

He turned back to the captain, but that individual was smoking in an unconcerned manner, as if nothing but of the ordinary had happened, and Blake decided that he would make no comment on the incident.

But before many days had passed he was to find that this was only the first of a very strange sequence of events at the cottage of the retired sea-captain.

THE SECOND CHAPTER.

The Murmurous Night.

WHEN Blake turned again the Celestial had disappeared as mysteriously and as silently as he had come. The old mariner (he had by then told Blake that his name was Corner —Captain Silas Corner —and somehow it had had a vaguely familiar ring to Blake's ears) was —still quite unconcerned, so Blake lit one of his own cigars and seated himself beside the young fellow who had been injured.

The captain excused himself, saying he would see about arrangements for the night, and for a little while Blake permitted the injured man to talk. It appeared that he was a clerk from a small town along the road which the Grey Panther would take on the way to London, and had been on his way to Exeter to spend the week-end with his parents when he had crashed into the car. It was Friday afternoon.

He was eager to assure Blake that it had been his own fault, and it was impossible for Blake to disagree, for that was nothing but the truth. He insisted that he was really well enough to be on his way. But Blake shook his head.

"Must obey doctor's orders." he said pleasantly. "We will stop and see him in the morning, and then drop you off at the town where you have been working. You will have to go to Exeter by train, I am afraid, as I cannot go back there now. I should have reached London to-night, as I have some business to attend to there."

"Oh, I'll be all right, sir," said the other. "I can go down by train, and I shall be very grateful to you if you will take me as far as Brinscombe. But, if possible. I'd like to save what remains of my bike."

"I'll speak to Captain Corner about that," promised Blake. "If he will take care of it here for you, I suppose you can get someone to pick it up for you?"

"Yes, sir. Our delivery cart comes out almost this far, and I can get the driver to bring it in for me."

Just then Tinker re-entered, and at sight of the lad Blake had an idea.

"I'll tell you what we will do," he said. "We will drive back along the road in my car and bring the bike back in it. We will have plenty of time before supper. And now try and doze. You need all the sleep you can get after that crack on the head."

The young fellow protested, but Blake laughed away his objections, and he and Tinker made their way into the kitchen. There was no sign of the Chinaman there, but as they reached the yard they saw the captain coming towards them. Blake explained where they were bound, and the old man promised he would look after the broken bike until it was called for, although he accompanied the promise by further disparaging remarks about such means of locomotion.

They found the wreckage lying just where it had landed after its pyrotechnic display of somersaults, and a couple of yokels were standing by, gazing at it stupidly. They were willing enough to give a hand with it into the tonneau of the Grey Panther, and equally willing to accept the couple of shillings which Blake gave them for their trouble. Then Tinker trundled the Grey Panther back to the farm, and by the time they were back in the house they could smell food cooking, although it seemed rather strange that the cooking was not being done in the kitchen, which one would ordinarily think ought to be used for that purpose. Nor did they see in what place it was being done.

The captain had been sitting beside the injured man, who was now asleep, and as they came in he whispered that he would show them their "berths." Tinker went back to get their bags, and they followed their host through the kitchen into a hall and up a narrow flight of steps to a floor above. The hall was almost in darkness, and there, as well as on the upper floor, there was a faint, indefinable perfume which reminded Blake of the East. What it was he could not say, and he told himself he probably imagined it after seeing the Chinese cook.

Their rooms adjoined, and were large chambers, plainly but well furnished, with large teak beds, teak washstands and wardrobes, and spotlessly clean, polished floors. The chairs were also of teak, and before each bed was a grass mat of Chinese manufacture. In the fireplace in each room a cheerful wood fire had been lighted, and the blaze was welcome, for although the day had been warm, almost summery, the nights were still cold.

The door between the two rooms was ajar, and while they freshened themselves up for supper, Blake and Tinker discussed the different phases of the accident. They went down together and made their way through the kitchen to the captain's "cabin," where they found he had changed from his rough clothes of the afternoon to a neat blue suit, the coat of which was cut double-breasted.

Specially light food was to be provided for the injured man, and when he had mentioned this their host led them along to what he was pleased to call the chart-room. They reached this through the kitchen again —the house was most peculiarly planned —and on entering, the first thing Blake and Tinker saw was a plain staircase, made exactly like a deck companionway, which led through a hole in the ceiling to a room above. At the moment a hatchway was closed over the aperture, and it was impossible to see through.

The "chart-room" itself was a bare, painted room, fitted up as nearly like the shipboard-room after which it took its name as was possible, with the exception that it was evident the captain took all his meals there. It was somewhat of a novelty to eat ashore in such surroundings, and both Blake and the lad found it pleasant.

And the dinner!

Blake caught the sniff of it before it was brought in, and, closing his eyes, he could quite easily imagine that he was back in Canton, supping at the Tavern of the Blue Peacock, which stands just inside the Gates of the Yellow Tiger and behind the Temple of Eternal Purity.

Whether the captain ever indulged in the food of his own country or not Blake did not know, for he did not ask. But it was evident that, like so many persons who have spent years in the Far East, he had brought back with him a love of the strange dishes of that part of the world, and with his Chinese cook it was easy enough for him to indulge his fancies, no doubt, although Blake wondered if he found it difficult to secure the various items which went to make up the lengthy and startling menu.

There was wine-vapour duck and kinkle chop-suey, why shon pigeon and lobster soaked in golden liquid, gold-cash chickens and tiger skin pigeon eggs trimmed with bamboo shoots. That much of the assortment —and it was only a portion of the extraordinary supper — Blake recognised, and Tinker knew some of them. Blake could trace, too, some of the ingredients, such as lily flower and the bamboo shoots, water chestnuts and bean sprouts, birds' nests, sesamum-seed oil and Chinese cabbage, not to mention wah mein and chow mein, with oceans of vegetables, and, of course, the rice which stood in a red-and-black lacquered bowl at one hand until the soya sweet was brought. And, finally, the delectable Chinese ginger, winding up with a glass of old, old brandy and the most intriguing of yellow cigarettes.

It was like a sudden plunge into the very inner regions of an exclusive Chinese house, and as they had trundled along the Devonshire lanes that afternoon, little did either of them dream that his evening meal was to be of that sort. At the house of Hong-Lo-Soo, the wealthy Chinese merchant of Packer's Court, in London, Blake had had Chinese meals before. But that was different. Here in this mediocre little farm in the heart of Devon he had plunged into one of the strangest places he had ever seen, a place tenanted by an equally strange master, and a servant with all the silent mystery of China still clinging to his appearance and movements.

And yet it was distinctly pleasant.

After supper —which took a good two hours to get through — they adjourned to the "cabin," and settled down to smoke and talk. During their absence the injured man had disappeared, and his host informed Blake that he had been changed to another room on the ground floor. Then they talked —talked of China and Indo-China, of Japan and Formosa, of the Philippines and New Guinea, of Siam and the Straits and India, of every port and every country fringing on the Seven Seas, and be sure Tinker came in with his share.

During the evening Blake had taken note several times of the various objects in the room, but one had particularly struck his fancy, and when at last the conversation languished he rose and walked across to a part of the room near the great, polished turtle-back shell. He bent over the object which interested him, and he studied it.

It was, or appeared to be, a red-lacquered table, which he now saw seemed to have an assortment of gilt characters on its surface. They were not very distinct, either, through the gilt having been rubbed off, or because they were dirt-grimed; he could not be sure in the poor light. He had seen a somewhat similar table once in Canton, and on that occasion he had been told that it was of considerable rarity and value. Hence, he was more than a little interested to find a table of similar appearance in the little sitting-room of that strange farmhouse in Devon. After a few moments he turned to his host.

"Rather an interesting object this, captain," he said. "I think I saw something like it once in Canton."

"Not unlikely, Mr. Blake," responded the mariner, hiding a yawn. "I was in the 1911 mix-up over there, and had a pretty hectic time, I can tell you. Brought away several refugees and their belongings, and that table was among them. I brought it along to Europe with me, and it has been stuck in that corner ever since. I don't think it is worth very much. Looks like a dirty bit of furniture to me."

"I am inclined to think it is worth more than you think," responded Blake. "I have a fairly, comprehensive collection of Chinese objets d'art, but I have nothing like this."

"You can have that if you want it. But I tell you it isn't worth much."

"I should be happy to add it to my collection, but I should not like to take it away from you, captain. You have been too good to stray travellers."

"You needn't worry about that. Name your own price for it if that will make you feel easier, and take it along with you in the morning. I don't want it."

"If you truly feel that way about it, why, then —well, I should like to make a suggestion, Captain Corner. Let me pay you an agreed figure, and then I shall write to a man who is, I know, an expert in such matters, and get his valuation on it. If it is more than I have paid I shall send you the balance at once."

"All right!" said the old mariner carelessly, and his tones said that the money didn't interest him very much. Nor need it have done so, for the old rascal had piled up a snug little fortune on the China Coast. "Pay what you think you want to, and leave it as you suggest."

So, after a little more friendly argument, they fixed on the price which Blake suggested —fifty pounds —although the captain insisted this was too much. Then, after a final pipe, they made ready to retire, Blake feeling pleased that the ill-chance that had brought him to the farm that day had some good in it, after all.

He and Tinker were both tired, so their good-night was brief, and, with a word as to what time he would be up in the morning, Blake closed the door which joined their rooms. He undressed quickly, and puffed a final cigarette before blowing out the light. The fire in the hearth had been replenished while they sat downstairs, and lit up the place with a pleasant flicker. The bed was wide and deep, and gave forth a faint, pleasant odour which soon lulled Blake into slumber, and it seemed that he had scarcely touched the sheets when a wonderful drowsiness stole over him, and he was off.

How long he had been asleep before he woke up Blake could not tell. The flames were still flickering in the fireplace, although the wood logs had dropped a little. He turned over lazily, and, punching the pillow, attempted to settle himself again. It was then he became aware of a low, persistent sort of murmur that seemed as if it might be coming from an adjoining room.

He paid no attention to it at first, but still tried to get back to sleep. But the tighter he pressed his head against the pillow the more discernible was the murmur as if the vibrations were rising from the floor through the bed. He turned twice, irritably. Then, suddenly, with a smothered exclamation, he sat up in bed. He slipped out from under the clothes and stole across to the chair, on the back of which he had hung his coat and waistcoat. He took out his gold repeater, and by the light of the fire glanced at the hands.

A quarter-past midnight! Only that, and it seemed to him as if he must have been asleep for several hours. They had come up to bed at a quarter to eleven, and he had fallen asleep soon after the hour, so that meant he had been slumbering for just a bit over an hour.

He laid the watch on the bedside table, and walked across to the home-woven rug which lay in front of the fireplace. He took a box of A-batschari cigarettes from the mantel and lit one. Then, as if through an afterthought, he pushed his feet into his bed-room slippers.

While he stood by the mantel, smoking, he listened. From there he could not hear the murmur which, it seemed, had wakened him. He "slush-slushed" over to the window, and, drawing the curtain aside, looked out. There was a bright moon, almost full, riding high in the sky, and from his window he could see a good distance across the fields. Somewhere a dog was howling, but in the farmyard below everything was as quiet and peaceful as could be.

He dropped the curtain and went back to the fire. Again he listened for some sound, but could hear nothing. Then, gradually, without any real sense of just when it began, he was aware of the same peculiar Eastern odour which had assailed his nostrils at dinner-time. What was it? He tried to think. It wasn't joss; he would have recognised that at once. It wasn't saffron. It wasn't kang-mein.

Was it in the room? He made a tour, taking care not to cause any noise; but he could find nothing from which the odour could emanate. He paused by the door which led to Tinker's room, and turned the handle ever so gently. He pushed the door open and peered in. As in his own room, a fire had been burning in the grate, and was still glowing. By it he could see the lad's form under the bedclothes, and just then a snore greeted his ears, which told him that Tinker, at least, had not been disturbed by anything.

Blake closed the door softly, and retreated into his own room. Then he stood close to his own bed, laid his head against the wood, and listened. Yes, there it was again, the same persistent murmur. He tried the wall, and again got the sound. He went along, step by step, in this way until he had reached the corner by the door which led out into the corridor. Here, as he laid his ear against the wall, he could hear the sound more distinctly than ever. He opened the door with infinite caution and stepped into the corridor.

He stood there, listening. And now the sound came to him more clearly than ever. He did not change his position, and then, as he strained his ears, he thought the murmur deepened to a deep bass. It sounded like the voice of his host, but a few moments later it changed to a high treble, a treble in which the inflection was odd and the nuance of tone strange.

Blake had no desire to spy on his host. That was the last thing he would have dreamed of doing, but he was more than curious. Living the life he had lived, he had become almost automatically attuned to the strange and the bizarre, and his subconsciousness was far more active in its urge than that of the ordinary person. There had been something queer about the atmosphere of the place that had intrigued him, and he could not forget the uncanny manner in which the Chinese cook had appeared and disappeared. In China he would not have thought much of that. But here, in this quiet farmhouse in Devon —well, it was different.

Then it suddenly occurred to him that perhaps the sound came from the injured man downstairs. What if he had developed a temperature, fever, was delirious? At that thought, and, judging from the silence that reigned over the house that no one else was awake, he determined to creep along the hall and down the stairs to see if the young fellow needed anything.

With this idea in his mind, Blake started, not bothering to go back for a dressing-gown, as the house was warm. He passed the corridor door of Tinker's room, and then a door on the same side and another door on the right. It was just then that he heard clearly the sound of voices behind that door, and he paused.

He figured the room there must be the one which the odd sort of companionway in the "chart" room had led to, which meant that it was the captain's bed-room, he supposed, for he figured that the "cabin" downstairs would only be used during the day. And now he heard his host's voice distinctly.

"No —no —no," he was saying, and then —silence.

But immediately that oddly pitched treble broke out again, and as Blake listened to it his trained ears told him it was the voice of no European. It was of the East, and as it seemed to take on a beseeching cadence he turned swiftly, angry with himself that he had apparently stumbled on some or the captain's private matters, which were none of his concern.

He shuffled back to his own room and gently closed the door after him.

He again approached the fire, and stood gazing into the flames.

"I'm sorry I worried about it," he muttered. "It is certainly my host's own affair if he wishes to remain up until this hour, and if we haven't met everyone who lives under this roof, what matters it? We are complete strangers to him, and his private arrangements are none of our business. I'll get back under the sheets and see if I can get to sleep."

And this time when he pressed his head on the pillow Blake no longer heard the murmur that had stirred him into wakefulness. He drowsed off almost at once, and his last conscious thought was that he would certainly sleep straight through until Tinker hammered on his door in the morning.

But in that thought he was vastly in error.

. . . a Chinese lady, seated on the floor just inside the room. By the glow
of the fire, Sexton Blake made out her most gorgeous robe, which fell about her
in gleaming folds as she sat there, statuesque. (*See this page.*)

An Exciting Night.

BLAKE woke the second time abruptly, as clear-headed as if he had not been asleep at all. And the same impulse that had brought him back to consciousness impelled him to sit up in bed.

His glance first fell on the fire, for it was directly in his line of vision. The flames had ceased, but the wood was glowing red, and that was sufficient to enable him to see about the room, although the corners and the space beyond the wardrobe were in shadow.

He listened, but heard nothing. The whole house seemed wrapped in utter silence. Yet he knew it was no dream that had roused him into wakefulness. He was quite certain of that, for his subconsciousness did not play him those sort of tricks.

Then what could it have been? It was something outside himself. But was it outside the room? Had it been a sound of some sort that had ceased as he woke? He looked towards the window, but the blind appeared just as he had left it, and there was the same faint swaying of the upper part of the chintz curtain, just as it had been before, clue to the fact that he had pulled the upper sash down a foot or so for ventilation.

Again he looked towards the fire. Nothing there. Now he put out his hand and shifted his position so as to reach for his watch, which was on the night-table at the left of the bed. His gaze came round in that direction, and as it did so he grew paralysed just as he sat at the sight which met his eyes.

Never in his life had Sexton Blake received a greater shock than at that moment. If anyone had asked him to suggest what had seemed to him the most bizarre situation that had ever arisen or could arise, what he was encountering at this moment was the last thing he should have thought of.

Remember, he was in an ordinary farmhouse down in Devon, and while there had been one or two odd things about the occupant and his strange way of living, that was not very remarkable when one paused to remember that he was a retired sea captain who had spent many years on the China coast, and who, like so many of his kind, could not have been happy ashore without collecting about him as many things as possible from the life he had known for so long, which had become an ingrained part of his nature. That had been sufficient explanation for Blake —up to then.

But now! Dear Heaven! Was he, after all, asleep, and had he not woke up at all? Was this just a fantastic dream that had filled his subconsciousness because he had indulged too freely in the extraordinary supper which his host had provided? He drew his hand back, and the physical touch as it came into contact with the bedclothes told him that it was no dream, but stark reality; and yet it seemed utterly impossible that he could be seeing what his eyes told him was there.

And what was it?

It was, as far as his amazed senses could make out, a Chinese lady seated on the floor just inside the room. A lady of the upper classes, because she was dressed as only the higher grades of Chinese women dress.

By the dull glow of the fire Blake made out a most gorgeous silk robe, which seemed to be of deep yellow and was decorated in a most exquisite way with a wonderful arrangement of crimson and blue and purple peacocks. She seemed to be sitting on her heels, her knees on the floor, and the heavy robe fell about her in gleaming folds.

Her hair was done high, every hair as smooth and as shining as polished ebony, and at the back three long jewelled jade pins which threw crisscross shadows on the wall behind her. Her face, Blake could see, was enamelled, and her brows lined with the black which high-class Chinese women use. Her lips were painted scarlet, and about her throat was a great topaz collar —the badge of those who mixed intimately in the life of the Imperial Court. He could not see her hands, for they were hidden in the loose folds of the sleeves of the gorgeous yellow robe. But he could see her eyes, and they were staring straight at him from beneath the arched brows. Sloe-black they were, or appeared to be in the soft light.

It is little wonder that Blake was startled. For once in his life he was utterly at a loss what to say, and it did not help matters any that the woman just sat looking at him without uttering a word. It was more than startling —it was decidedly embarrassing.

At last Blake decided he would have to do something. He reached down to the foot of the bed, where he had thrown a flowered silk dressing-gown, and got his arms into it. Then he got out of bed, put on his slippers, and as he came to his feet drew his dressing-gown about him. Then, feeling more capable of tackling such an extraordinary situation, he walked round the bed and stood before her.

Blake knew his China and the customs well enough to know that without question this woman before him was not masquerading. There could not be the slightest doubt but that she was what she appeared to be. And that was what made the puzzle all the more intriguing, for certainly a high-class Chinese lady is not customarily to be found, in the most gorgeous of formal robes, squatting on the floor of a bed-room in a farmhouse in Devonshire.

Blake placed his hands across the front of his body —the seat of wisdom and the most-to-be-respected part —and bowed gravely. Then, using his very best and most flowery Cantonese, he spoke, taking good care to keep his voice scarcely above a whisper. It is not necessary here to repeat all the usual flowery phrases which he employed, but the gist of what he said and what she replied was about this, taking it as a free translation.

"Honourable lady, you are most gracious to honour me with your presence," said Blake. "My unworthy ears are attuned to hear your gracious words."

The woman, who, Blake saw now that he was close to her, was young, and, from an Eastern point of view —or any point of view, for that matter —extremely beautiful, bent forward rapidly until her forehead touched the floor. A second and a third time she made this obeisance; then, with her sloe eyes fastened on Blake's, she spoke. And as he heard her soft, fluty voice Blake knew it was the same oddly-pitched treble which he had heard in Captain Corner's room.

"My lord," she said, "why hast thou come here? Forgive my not-to-be-counted anxiety. But when wilt thou go away, my lord?"

Blake was puzzled. He had been searching for a lead, and now he had it. For some reason or other his presence in the place had upset her, and she had been so driven by this anxiety that she had come to his room to make a personal plea to him. Why?

"You will forgive me, honourable lady, but I did not know that my unworthy feet had carried me here as an unwelcome guest. Had I known that I should not have entered. But peace be unto you, honourable lady, for I leave to-morrow morning."

Again she made obeisance three times; then:

"Thou art gracious, my lord. Wilt thou grant me one favour, even unto one whom thou mayest tread beneath your honourable feet?"

"What is it that thou seekest?"

"My lord, thou hast made purchase of a certain object here to-night. I would that thou choosest anything else but that. May the light of the wise Confucius illuminate thy mind and put other wishes into it."

"Um!"

Blake was almost unconscious that he had uttered the very Anglo-Saxon grunt. So this was it, he was thinking. He had made a purchase, and she didn't want him to take it away.

Well, the only thing he had purchased was the red lacquered table with the dusty gold characters on the top. So it must be that. But why? Who the dickens was she, anyway? And why should she get so exercised over his purchase? Was that what she had been talking about to the captain? And when he had heard the latter say, "No, no, no!" was he refusing to ask his guest to cancel the agreement they had made?

This was what he was thinking as he gazed down at her. And he knew, too, that, whatever it was, it must have exercised her very deeply indeed to make her come to make a personal appeal, as she had done; for it is a most unheard-of thing for a high-class Chinese lady to do such a thing. And it is only natural that Blake, knowing as much as he did of China, should wonder why she was so anxious. Perhaps the table had been her property and had great value in her eyes, having belonged to some ancestor. But, whatever it was, he did not want the table if it were going to make her or any woman unhappy. And he said so, even though he was disappointed at losing the chance to add it to his collection.

"Fear not, honourable lady," he said quietly. "You speak of the table which I purchased —is it not so?"

Her head bowed in acquiescence.

"I shall tell my host to-morrow that I do not want it, after all. It shall remain here. You have my promise."

As he finished speaking she again made that triple obeisance; and then, much to Blake's embarrassment, caught hold of his hand and pressed it against her forehead.

"I am my lord's slave," she said humbly. "My lord may command of me what he will."

"Rise, honourable lady, and fear not," said Blake, decidedly nonplussed at her fervent gratitude. "It shall be as I say."

But what he intended saying died in his throat as a sudden racket broke out in Tinker's room. At first he thought the lad must have fallen out of bed, for there was a heavy thud and then a scrambling sound. But a few moments later Blake heard something that sounded like a chair go over with a crash, and he dropped the woman's hand. He was not so sure now that it had been the table that had brought her to his room at that hour of the night —or, rather, morning. He was acutely suspicious, and he covered the distance from where he stood to Tinker's door, in two strides.

He caught hold of the handle and wrenched the door open. He plunged into the room, saying as he did so:

"What is it, my lad? What is wrong?"

But he got no answer, and the open door into the corridor told him that the lad was not in the room. The wood was still glowing in the fireplace, and Blake could see that the bedclothes had been thrown off hurriedly, for they hung half on the floor.

Just then another racket broke out in the corridor, and he ran to the door. As he reached it he heard Tinker's voice exclaiming in anger; and then, as he burst out, he saw two dim figures struggling some distance along. He raced in that direction, and had almost reached what he now saw were two struggling figures, when all of a sudden they disappeared, and there was a terrific clatter as they went hurtling down the stairs.

Blake tore down after them, and at the bottom collided with Tinker, who was scrambling to his feet. He lit into Blake like a tornado until at last Blake's voice penetrated through the rage under which he was labouring. Tinker drew back, panting.

"What on earth is it, my lad?" asked Blake. "What has happened?"

"Was it you I was fighting with all the time, then?" asked Tinker. "I could have sworn it was a Chink. Were you in my room? Did I have a nightmare and take you for a Chink?"

"I certainly was not in your room," answered Blake. "And just as certainly you were fighting with someone else. Tell me what happened. But, first, come back upstairs. I don't know what our host will think of all this racket. It is a wonder to me he hasn't come out to see what is wrong. But wait! There is our young friend calling. He is probably thinking burglars have broken in. Wait here until I reassure him."

With that Blake went along the lower hall, and after tapping on the door of the room where the injured man was sleeping, opened it. A small night-light was burning on a table beside the bed, and he could see the young fellow sitting up, looking startled.

"It's all right!" Blake said, with a laugh. "Sorry you were woke up. My assistant must have had a nightmare, or was walking in his sleep. He fell down the stairs."

"Oh!" said the other, with a breath of relief. "I didn't know what was up. I hope he isn't hurt?"

"Not a bit. I shall put him back into bed now. Try and get to sleep. Good-night again!"

And with that Blake retreated.

He made his way back to where Tinker was waiting, and the pair went up the stairs. At the top Blake touched the lad's arm and paused by the door which he took to be the one opening into their host's room. He listened, and his face registered surprise as he heard heavy snores coming from the other side. Still, he decided to wake him and explain things, in case the injured man should mention the incident in the morning. So he knocked. The snores did not alter, so he knocked again and then again. But, despite the racket he made, the snores continued just the same, and after a last heavy assault on the door Blake gave it up.

But he was thinking as they went along to Tinker's room:

"That man is either in a drunken sleep or a drugged stupor!"

Once in Tinker's room, he motioned to the lad to close the door, while he hurried over to the door leading to his own room and looked through. He had no desire just then for Tinker to see the strange sight which had greeted him on waking the last time.

But he need not have worried, for the room was quite empty, and now it was difficult to believe that she had ever been there —or would have been so if it weren't for the persistent, subtle odour which he had noticed before, and which had by now penetrated into Tinker's room.

Blake strode across his room and caught up the box of A-batscharis and some matches. Then he returned, to find Tinker sitting on the side of his bed. The lad had lit the lamp, and by its light Blake could see a nasty red bruise on his neck.

"Are you sure you are not hurt?" asked the detective quickly.

"I feel all right, guv'nor," answered Tinker slowly. "But I am darned if I know what to think. I don't seem to be awake even yet."

"Judging from the way you were scrapping, you were wide awake enough," remarked Blake. "But tell me just what happened."

"Well, sir, I was fast asleep when something woke me. I opened my eyes, and I felt as if someone was pressing down on me. I couldn't seem to breathe. I must have been only partially awake. Anyway, I tried to throw off whatever it was, and then I felt a pair of hands at my throat. I managed to twist over, and, by ginger, what did I find but a Chink trying to throttle me!

"I brought up one knee and gave it to him in the stomach, and as his hold broke I threw myself out of bed. Then I went for him. I caught him a peach on the jaw, and landed another to the body, and he tried to get away. He reached the door and got it open; but I was on the jump after him, and tackled him in the corridor.

"Well, sir, I guess you know the rest. I didn't know the stairs were so close —had forgotten about them —and away we went down them before I could stop myself. Then you landed on the job; but — but, guv'nor, what the dickens did become of that Chink?"

"I can't tell you, my lad," answered Blake in a puzzled tone. "You were most certainly fighting with someone! It was no ghost, and I saw the pair of you go down the stairs. I was after you not two seconds later, and yet I did not see the other person get away, or even hear him go. He must have vanished the moment he struck bottom."

"But I tell you I was hanging on to him until the moment we hit the ground," protested the lad. "I was just reaching out to grab him again when I caught hold of you. But even at that, whom could it have been, guv'nor? Why should any of Captain Corner's Chinks —I suppose it was one of his —try to throttle me?"

"Do you think it was the cook —the same man who waited at table?" asked Blake quickly.

"No, sir, I don't. He was a flatter-faced bird than that."

"Well, now listen, Tinker. You are not the only one who has had a strange experience to-night. I have had my share of them, but I shall tell you about that to-morrow. In the meantime, I want you to say nothing about it either to the young fellow downstairs or to Captain Corner. If I could have roused him I should have told him, as a matter of duty, but now, there are reasons why, unless he broaches the subject, I shall say nothing. Do you understand?"

"Of course, guv'nor. What you say goes with me. But, just the same, I'd like to know what happened to you. And what became of that Chink?"

"To-morrow, when we are on the road to London, I shall tell you what happened to me," promised Blake. "As for the Chink who attacked you, we shall let that drop for the present. We shall get back to bed now; but, before doing so, I shall lock both doors leading into the corridor, and leave the communicating door open. Also, we shall keep our pistols handy. While I lock the doors, you get them out."

Ten minutes later they were once more back in bed, and this time Blake fervently hoped he would not be disturbed again. Nor was he until Tinker came into his room at seven o'clock.

But before dropping off to sleep Blake's mind was still working on the strange events of the evening, and it was just when he was on the point of losing consciousness that he found the answer to one of the questions which he had been asking himself.

He was thinking about the strange odour which he had whiffed again and again —that elusive, subtle odour. And suddenly he knew.

It was opium!

THE FOURTH CHAPTER.

A Bargain is a Bargain.

BLAKE and Tinker descended at eight o'clock, and found the injured cyclist already up and dressed, and sitting in the "cabin." He looked much better, and expressed himself as quite fit to move along when they were ready. There was no sign of their host at the moment, and Blake took the opportunity to mention to the young fellow that it would be as well to say nothing to the captain about the noise in the night, since he had apparently not heard it, and it would do no good to bring it up.

To this the other readily agreed, for he was more than grateful to Blake and Tinker for what they had done for him; and, besides, he had a vast respect for the great criminologist. It would be a never-ending story of his, how he had spent a night in the company of the pair.

Shortly after that Captain Corner came thumping in on his wooden leg. Blake greeted him cheerfully, but as he looked at him took careful note of his face. That one look was all he needed. He knew now why the captain had not been roused by the row in the night, for Blake had seen the after-signs of an opium bout far too often not to be able to recognise them at a glance. And that, too, confirmed his guess at the odour which had puzzled him for so long the night before.

They went into breakfast almost at once, the meal being in sharp contrast to the supper of the night before, consisting as it did of bacon and eggs and the other appurtenances of the regular English breakfast. The captain seemed moody, and not much inclined for conversation, so Blake, Tinker, and the other young fellow kept the ball rolling between them. Blake could guess that the captain must have a terrific "head," and he sympathised with him.

The cook waited on them at table, but one could never have told from his impassive face whether he knew anything of the events of the night or not, although Blake, naturally, had him under surveillance. But not even Blake, in the wildest of guesses, would have hit on the truth. And certainly he never for a single moment thought that the same yellow hand which passed him his bacon had rammed an eight-inch blade into a man's heart during the night. Nor would he have guessed that, at that very moment, the body of a dead Chinaman was lying beneath a heap of sacks in one of the outhouses. There was a lot about this Devonshire homestead Blake had yet to learn.

After breakfast they adjourned to the "cabin" for a smoke, and to take leave of their host. There the captain got out the lacquered table and began to wipe it off before having it put in the car. Blake seized this opportunity to say:

"About the table, captain. I have been thinking over what we agreed on. If it is all the same to you. I think it would be better if I got the opinion of the expert before I take it away. Then, you see, I could write you just what he says; and, if the price struck you as being fair, why then we could make the deal."

The captain went on wiping the table. He neither looked up nor turned round. But after a few moments he said gruffly:

"You and I made a deal last night didn't we, Mr. Blake?"

"Quite correct."

"And you paid me fifty pounds, didn't you?"

"I did."

"Then the incident is closed so far as I am concerned, and the table goes with you. If the expert you consult says it is worth as much as you have already paid me, then you can, if you wish, let me know the difference. On the other hand, if you want your fifty pounds back you can have it; but, in any case, the table goes with you this morning, or, if you haven't room in your car for it, it will fellow you by rail. With me a deal is a deal, and, by the great horned toad, the table is your property, and that settles it!"

Tinker, who up to now knew nothing yet of what had happened in Blake's bed-room the night before, looked up in surprise at his master. He was curious to know why Blake had suddenly switched over in this way. He knew that Blake had been as keen as mustard the evening before to get hold of the table, and had been more than pleased with the terms of the bargain he had made with his host.

Then why this sudden about-turn, the lad was wondering. He put it down to the fact that Blake must have some idea in his head that it would be a pity to take the table away from the captain after he had had it so many years, for that was the sort of feeling that would influence his master.

As for Blake, he gazed about him helplessly. He could not, either alone or in front of the others, explain why he had changed his mind, nor could he make any mention of what he had overheard going on in the captain's room before he had succumbed to the fumes of the opium he must even then have been smoking. And something in the attitude of his host —in the way in which he occupied himself over the table and did not turn round —warned Blake that his instinct was right.

It told him, too, that, whatever the reason, the captain was determined to stick to his bargain. And yet there was the promise he had practically made to the woman. What should he do? What could he do?

If the captain insisted on the table being put in the car it would be quite impossible for him to go to the extent of a quarrel over it. The thing would appear altogether too churlish after having accepted the bountiful hospitality of the man. He could, he figured inwardly, take the thing along with him if necessary, and either hit on some scheme to send it back after he had heard from the expert, or else convey to the woman in some way that it would be perfectly safe in his care. What on earth she wanted with it, or why she put such terrific value on it, he hadn't the remotest notion.

But that there was some tremendous purpose which had impelled her to visit his room in the night he was certain. It might be real or imaginary, but Chinese ladies of high degree do not do that sort of thing, and her gratitude had been so great that it had been embarrassing. He made one more attempt to get his way.

"I understand how you feel, captain," he said pleasantly, "but I assure you I shall have no thoughts such as you suggest if we call the bargain off, or, alternatively, do as I have suggested. It will crowd the car a bit; and as for sending it up by rail —why, I shouldn't care to risk having it banged about on the railway"

The captain snorted.

"I'll see that it is well wrapped up in straw and burlap," he said. "If you don't want to take it in the car, then it goes by train. When I make a bargain it stays made. And you did not strike me as the type of man who would want to back out of one, Mr. Blake. I'll give you back your fifty pounds before you go."

Blake surrendered. There was nothing else he could do.

"Oh. all right, captain, have it as you wish," he said, with a laugh. "We will get it into the car some way. And by the same token I think

26

it is time we were making a start. I have a lot of work waiting to be attended to in London."

So, despite his strategy —or lack of it —Blake was forced to stand by while the captain personally piled the red-lacquered table into the tonneau. The young fellow whom they were to drop at the next village took his place beside it, and kept a hand against it in order to steady it.

Then when Blake and Tinker had warmly thanked their host for his hospitality, and had extended an invitation to him to visit them in London, they also got in, Tinker taking the wheel.

Just before they drove out of the farmyard Blake saw the Chinese cook come out on to the porch and look in their direction. He had given the man a good tip, but could not tell at the time whether he had been pleased with it or not. Nor was there the slightest sign to hint whether the cook knew anything of the strange events of the night or not. He just stood there on the porch, as motionless and as expressionless of feature as a yellow idol, and he was still standing there when the car drove off.

As Tinker swung into the drive which led to the road, Blake turned round to wave his hand to the captain. As he did so his eyes raked the south side of the house, and he was almost sure he saw a blind drawn down sharply.

"Someone," he thought, "is in that room upstairs watching our departure. I wonder if it is the strange lady who visited me in the night? I'd give a good deal to know the meaning of the mystery which surrounds that place," his thoughts went on. "I wonder just how much the captain knows —if he knows anything?

"If is certainly a strange house. There is the old sea-dog, with his one good leg and his one wooden leg, living in that isolated farm here in Devon, with the interior of the place made as much like a ship as he can get it. There isn't a single European servant anywhere inside, and, as far as I have seen, there isn't a European farmhand outside either. What work is done on the place must be done by casual labour or by the captain and his Chink cook. I don't see many signs of crops, or even of cattle, so I don't suppose there is much to do.

"And on top of that the captain is a 'hophead.' If I hadn't smelt that opium last night I could almost have guessed the truth from his eyes this morning. He picked that up, of course, in China, just as my friend Hsui-fsi" (Sir Gordon Saddler, the Mystery Man of 'Frisco) picked it up. But the woman. In what relation does she stand to the captain, and what is she doing there?

"She is of high birth. Of that I am sure. Aside from the clothes she was wearing she had the manner, and in her own country she would not be on terms of equality with a coast captain. And yet she was pleading with him about something last night, and I am willing to wager it was about the lacquered table which is in the back of the car. It is a mighty queer mix-up there; but, after all, it is none of my business.

"Heigh-ho! It is a darned funny world, and the longer I live the more I see to puzzle me. As Tinker would vulgarly put it, you never can tell where a pimple will start!"

And with that Blake tried to dismiss the whole business from his mind.

But he would have been less anxious to do so had he known about the dead Chinaman who lay under the sacking in the outhouse behind them, and even less if he dreamed for a single moment that as they turned into the main road three pairs of sloe-black eyes were watching them —watching them, and at the same time taking careful note of the table in the back, of their own personal appearance, and of the licence number of the Grey Panther.

THE FIFTH CHAPTER.

The Empress' Little Finger.

FROM the farm they drove along to the village, some five miles distant, where they dropped the motorcyclist at the doctor's house.

From there he was to make his own arrangements, so after bidding him good-bye, and when Blake had delivered a little homily on the perils of reckless driving —a lecture which made Tinker grin, considering the pace at which Blake often drove the Grey Panther — they started on again, and as they were anxious to get to London as soon as possible, Tinker sent the car along at a rattling pace.

It was then, when he had got a cigar going, that Blake told the lad what had taken place the night before. He related first how he had been awakened by the sound of murmuring, which he identified as voices somewhere in the house, and finally tracked to the room which he thought the captain occupied. Then he told how he had awakened a second time to find the strange apparition of the young and beautiful Chinese lady sitting on the floor of his room.

"I don't know just what else she would have said," he remarked when he had finished. "That row in your room broke off the interview, and when I got back to my room she was gone. There is something queer about the attack on you, my lad. I can't seem to find any reasonable explanation for it. You do not think it was the cook, and it certainly wasn't the lady. We did not see any other Chinese about the place, although that does not say they were not there."

"Well, there must have been another," said Tinker thoughtfully. "I've been thinking that business over, guv'nor, and I am just as certain this morning as I was last night that it wasn't the cook. That cook has smallish features for a Chink, and this bird who jumped me in the night was very flat-faced. I could see that much."

"It is a most puzzling thing," agreed Blake. "It is the motive which I cannot understand. I think I am right in suspecting that the reason the captain was not roused by the noise was because he was in a drugged stupor. Someone, at any rate, was using opium in the house last night, and his eyes have a tell-tale look this morning."

"I noticed that all right. Do you think he knows about the visit the lady paid you, guv'nor?"

Blake frowned at the expression, but answered:

"I shouldn't think so for one moment. At the same time I feel convinced that she talked with him about the table last night. It is my theory that she went to him first and begged him not to let it go. You will remember that I told you I had heard him repeating a refusal several times. It is possible that he was referring to the table then."

"But why should she get so worked up over that old lacquered table?" asked the lad.

"Heavens, Tinker, I haven't the least idea! If I knew that, I might be able to explain a lot of things that are puzzling me. In order to build a theory round that we should have to know more about her. It would be interesting to know just what position she occupies in the household, and how she ever managed to get there. I should think it quite ordinary to find a high-caste Chinese lady in the house of Hong-Lo-Soo, our Chinese merchant friend, for example; or at the Chinese Embassy. But there in that lonely farm in Devon —in that house of that old mariner —it is, I confess, beyond me."

"He certainly acted queer about the table when you tried to call off the deal, guv'nor," remarked the lad at the end of another mile.

Blake nodded.

"What will, you do?" persisted Tinker.

"I haven't quite decided yet. I intend getting an expert opinion on it first. Then I shall make up my mind. If I could I would hand it over to the lady; but if that does not prove an easy matter, I shall let her know in some way that I shall take care of it for her until she wishes to claim it. That might develop into a delicate mission for you to handle, my lad, so that she gets the message and the captain does not suspect. Something has made him pigheaded over the business, and it is useless to waste any more time arguing with him. In any case, I shall not dispose of it to anyone else."

They talked over other phases of the business on the way, and made one brief halt for lunch. Then they were off again, and it was early afternoon when Tinker finally pulled up into the kerb at Baker Street. As it was uncertain whether they should need the car again or not, it was decided that Tinker should drive round to the garage and fill up with petrol, bringing the car back to the house in case Blake should want to use it.

In the meantime, Blake mounted the steps and entered. Mrs. Bardell had evidently been on the lookout for them, for she appeared as soon as he was inside the door. She followed Blake into the consulting-room, where he at once saw a big pile of envelopes on the flap of his desk. There was a second pile of telegrams, and while he opened and scanned these, he listened to the housekeeper's report of how things had gone during his absence. Then he told her to bring tea, and, throwing aside his coat and hat, sat down at his desk to give the telegrams more careful attention.

With the exception of one or two, they could all be attended to in routine manner by Tinker. The exceptions —some in code —Blake set to work on at once, and as he made a rough translation of each, he would lay it aside for Tinker to check before making a record of the contents, or asking Blake what should be done about it. Blake was so employed when the lad came in, and Tinker noticed that he was using the private code-book, which meant that Blake was working on a telegram that had come through either from one of their agents or correspondents, or else from some one of the few outside persons who was in possession of the private code.

As a matter of fact, it was from a person whose name Blake had mentioned in the car on the way up, and he was intensely engrossed as he took out the meaning of word after word. It was from Sir Gordon Saddler, and the first glance had shown Blake that it had been filed at San Francisco two days before. Which meant that it had been lying in the consulting-room since the previous morning.

It was a fairly long message, and Blake was a considerable time in decoding it; but at last he finished, and then he lit a cigarette and leant back to read it. This is how it ran:

"Sexton Blake,

"Baker Street,

"London.

"Recall to your mind our conversation two years ago in Canton, when I told you story of the little finger of the late Dowager-Empress of China. You probably have notes or recollection.

"Have, just been informed that Pu-Yi, the deposed Boy-Emperor of China, has escaped from the Palace of Cloudless Heaven with his young bride, and has reached the Japanese Legation. This took place some weeks ago, but has only just been disclosed. Have been credibly informed that persons working at direction of interests whose identity will be plain to you, are making every effort to locate and get possession of the empress' little finger.

"As I told you, it is believed to be somewhere in England, and these persons must be in England now. If they secure the relic it will complicate things badly, for it must be preserved and handed to Pu-Yi only, if we can secure it. Will you please make very special efforts to locate these people and foil their purpose. They are all Black Valley Tong men, so you will realise they will stop at nothing to gain their ends.

"Hong-Lo-Soo, your blood-brother and mine in the Four Lakes Tong may know something fresh. Advise you to get in touch with him. Please cable me sharp if you will use your efforts in this matter, and, if so, keep me advised of progress. Needless to add, you can name your own fee. If you require any funds or anything else, draw on Hong-Lo-Soo to any limit you wish. Salaams.

"HSUI-FSI."

Blake read over the remarkable cablegram a second and then a third time. He got up, and, walking across to Tinkers desk, laid it before him.

"Read that, my lad," he said curtly.

Tinker did so; then he looked up.

"I don't quite get it, guv'nor. What is all this about the empress' little finger?"

"I don't think I told you what Sir Gordon told me, my lad. But it is in my Chinese notebook. Dig that up and read what I have jotted down. Afterwards, I shall run through it again myself, just to refresh my memory. But, if I remember rightly, it is a matter of considerable importance, especially to Pu-Yi, the young boy emperor of China, who was dethroned in the revolution of 1911."

"Nineteen-eleven! That was the business Captain Corner was mixed up in," remarked Tinker. "Don't you remember him saying so yesterday evening?"

"Now that you come to mention it, I do," replied Blake. "What about it?"

"Nothing. I was just thinking of the coincidence of that date coming up two days running. What are you going to do about this 'gram, guv'nor?"

"I shall see Hong-Lo-Soo."

"Good egg. That looks as if we might get some action. Hong-Lo-Soo usually provides us with a little excitement. When do we go?"

"This evening, if we can catch him at home. And now get on with those other telegrams, my lad. We will talk this over when we have cleared the decks."

Chinks on the Brain.

IT must be recorded that Blake permitted Tinker to do most of the swotting at the routine work after tea. He indulged in what looked to Tinker like a good deal of wasted energy, for he got a large piece of chamois leather from the laboratory, and began to rub up the lack-lustre lacquer and the dusty gold characters on the top of the table, which had been the cause of so much mystery.

Tinker could not see the use in this idleness when he himself was up to his ears in letters and telegrams. But Blake paid no attention to the lad's scathing glances, and went on with his amusement, alternately puffing at a cigarette or whistling some ten-year-old music-hall ditty.

But Blake was far from indulging in aimless labour. Ever since the night before he had been thinking a good deal about the red-lacquered table, and he knew enough about China and the Chinese to realise that only something which, to her, must have been of the utmost importance, could have driven that Chinese lady to come to him as she had.

Her one and only plaint had been the table. Ergo, the table might give up the answer up the puzzle. So Blake kept on with his work, polishing away at the surface, and each moment bringing the dusty gold into higher relief, and at the same time revealing that it was a piece of workmanship far more exquisite than he had guessed.

The characters were confined to the top, although the gold decoration had been carried out on the rails of the table and the legs as well. But here it was in the form of scrolls and dragons, just conventional decoration. As he proceeded, Blake began to distinguish the characters as actual symbols in the Chinese language, characters of the classical grade, and, therefore, known only to the highly educated.

Now, in that written form of Chinese there are something like two hundred and twenty-six letters or forms, and the percentage of persons in China who know all those forms sufficiently well to understand the five classics is very small. The average rag-tag and bobtail do not comprehend them any more than the average man in the street in England can understand old Greek.

But in his study of the Chinese language and literature, Blake had devoted a vast amount of time to mastering every phase of the written language, and it had been said by Hsui-fsi and Hong-Lo-Soo, as well as by others, that his knowledge and understanding was superior to that possessed by many high-class mandarins. At any rate, Blake knew enough to read Confucius in the original tomes, and that is saying a good deal.

Therefore, it was not strange that, as he proceeded with his rubbing, he saw that, what seemed in the beginning to be just isolated characters of the written language, inlaid in the form of decoration, should turn out to appear to have some consecutive order, and as letter after letter, or, rather, character after character, became clear, he grew more and more engrossed in his work.

He read one whole line, but while he knew each word, he could not make sense of it. Then another line was revealed, and he linked this up with the first, trying to see what he could make from the two when studied together. But still it appeared without meaning. A third line gave no more result, and a fourth confused him more than ever. If there was such a thing in Chinese as blank verse he would have taken it for that, and sheer meaningless doggerel in addition.

But he persevered with the fifth and sixth lines, and then he set to work on the seventh and last. With the whole top cleaned, and the faded gold characters looking very, very beautiful against the deep red lacquer, it was certainly a very fine bit of work, and, apart from everything else, he knew, as he looked at it, that he had paid Captain Corner far less than its worth to any collector.

But he was not thinking of that then. He was still pondering over those confusing lines of characters, trying to drag some sort of sense out of them.

Now and then he seemed to get something that reminded him of one of the Chinese funeral chants, but then it would tail off into something which held no meaning at all. He went to his bookcase, and after some search took down a very rare volume on ciphers and cryptograms.

He was a master of this subject, and had himself written three monographs on various phases of the science. He had barely touched on Chinese cryptograms, however, for that in itself was a thing requiring years of study. He knew roughly of what type they were, and he knew that to understand them one had, first of all, to know what keyword was used. That never appeared in the cryptogram, and hence a Chinese cryptogram is not amenable to the same sort of solution which can be applied to other forms.

It might be such a thing, he reasoned. He sought through the book until he came to a section dealing with Chinese forms of the subject, and he went through this carefully. There were scores of examples of cryptograms that had actually been employed at one time or another, but there was nothing from one end to the other that gave the slightest hint regarding a type such as he was looking for.

And yet, somehow, he had a "hunch" that it was just that he had uncovered with that chamois rag. If it were, then it was one that had been invented for this single purpose and for nothing else. It would have been born and had died in the same moment, so to speak. But someone must know the keyword, and the person knowing that would know the secret of those characters.

Was that possible? Was that the reason why the Chinese lady had pleaded with him to leave the table behind? If so, what was its secret —her secret? To what did it refer? And if that were the case, did Captain Corner know anything about it? Blake decided that he couldn't, and if he didn't, then, for some reason, the woman had not told him. Of course, this might all be sheer random theory, but if it were not, then the secret of those characters on the top of the table might explain more than one riddle.

Again Blake applied himself to a concentrated analysis of the characters, taking each one slowly and with the utmost care, applying to it every phase and nuance he could think of. In this way he once more covered line after line until he reached the last. So far, he had found nothing that was at all suggestive, and as he came to the very last character in the seventh line he thought that he had drawn a blank.

Ninety-nine men out of a hundred would have given less concentration to the very last symbol. It is just the way the average mind works, and Blake knew from experience that this was so. But he did not relax a single jot of his attention even there; and as he went over in his mind every single thing he thought the character could refer to, he suddenly found himself thinking of something which made him pause and consider.

The idea was nothing more or less than that the character could refer to two things —one being Daughter of Heaven and the other

Palace of Cloudless Heaven.

It is difficult for a Western mind to grasp the intricacies of this, for, in English, our words are first made up of letters, and these in turn, by usage and selection, have come to refer to things of a single group or class. But in Chinese, as in many Oriental languages, one symbol, word, or phrase may refer to any number of things, having absolutely no relation one to the other. And this was why the whole thing which Blake was studying was so confusing, and more especially so as, if it were a cryptogram, he had no idea what the keyword might be, for that would not be found among the characters.

But these two things to which the last symbol might refer. What of them? Had they anything to do with the real meat of it, so to speak? Daughter of Heaven and Palace of Cloudless Heaven!

One meant a royal woman, and of recent years there had only been one woman ruler in China, the late Dowager Empress, who had ruled with a rod of iron, and had been feared and at the same time regarded as of Divine origin. Palace of Cloudless Heaven was one of the royal palaces in the sacred city in Pekin, and was one of the royal residences. It was there young Pu-Yi, the dethroned boy Emperor had been living until he had managed to escape.

Blake rubbed his chin thoughtfully and walked across to Tinker's desk, where the decoded draft of Sir Gordon Saddler's cable lay. He picked this up and read it again. Then he walked to the window and looked out into the street. As he did so he saw a man lurking in a doorway on the other side of the street, and as Blake held the curtain aside the fellow moved away and slunk along in the direction of Orchard Street. Blake thought little of the incident at first, except that the man's movements were of a suspicious nature, and it was the type of thing which his profession had taught him to observe almost mechanically.

It was almost dusk then, but he could see well enough to make out the fellow's features, and, as he turned his head a trifle, Blake caught a view of a flat-nosed profile that brought him suddenly to attention. For he was almost certain the man was a Chinaman!

He walked back to the table and regarded it once more. He turned it over and searched about for a considerable time, trying to find if it possessed a secret panel of any sort. But this yielded nothing, and he gave it up. He could have settled that question easily enough with a hatchet, but he would not go to such measures, for he really did not regard the table as his property, but as something he was holding in trust for the Chinese lady, according to his promise.

But the more he studied those characters —the more he pondered on the last symbol in the seventh line —the more they impinged upon his mind, beside his thoughts about what had occurred the previous night; and the more he puzzled over Hsui-fsi's cablegram the more was he beginning to think that in some way he had stumbled upon something that was far deeper than it had appeared at the farm.

Was it possible, he was asking himself, that this table had anything to do with Sir Gordon Saddler's cable? Could it have any reference to the Empress' Little Finger? If so, then what part was the Chinese lady of Devonshire playing in the affair? Was she for or against Pu-Yi, the boy emperor? For it was easy enough for Blake to see that, now he was free, Pu-Yi would deem it his first and most sacred duty to seek until he found the Empress' Little Finger. Only those who know the intensity of Chinese ancestor worship can understand this. And what was this about the Empress' Little Finger, as Tinker had asked? That was to be revealed a little later to the lad.

Blake gave it up then, but he was still determined to go round and see Hong-Lo-Soo, the Chinese merchant, in Packer's Court.

It was his intention to drive round in the Grey Panther after dinner, and for this reason he got into a dinner jacket, telling Tinker to do the same. They dined early, and then, as soon as they had had coffee in the consulting-room, Blake rose. He had been telling Tinker at dinner about the Chinaman he thought he had seen slinking along the other side of the street, and, taking one thing with another, Tinker, to use his own words, was getting Chinks on the brain.

He made this remark as he rose to get his coat and cap, but at that moment there was a ring at the street doorbell, and, as Blake knew Mrs. Bardell was busy in the basement with the dinner dishes, he told the lad to go along and answer the ring. Tinker trotted along the hall and opened the door. Blake was in the act of lighting a cigar when he heard Tinker's voice raised urgently.

"Come here —quickly, guv'nor!" he called, and Blake, tossing aside the match, opened the door and went along. He reached the front stoop to find Tinker bending over something on the top step, and then, as the lad moved aside a little, Blake saw what it was.

It was a Chinaman with a knife sunk in the back of his neck close to the spinal vertebrae. Blood was gushing from his mouth and nose, and it looked as if he had been killed instantaneously. But as Blake caught him by the shoulders the man made a convulsive movement and caught him by the arm.

Blake bent down until his ear was close to the stricken creature's lips, and he caught, ever so faintly, a few choking words in Chinese. So thickened was the utterance by the blood that was gushing from the throat that Blake could not be quite sure what they were, but they sounded like:

"The Sacred Finger of the Daughter of Heaven."

He still bent close, for the poor fellow was trying to speak again; but before he could do so a fresh flow of blood choked him, he gave one convulsive shudder, and then sank down like a sack of meal. Blake knew he had died in that last convulsion.

He signed to Tinker to give him a hand. They carried him into the consulting-room and laid him on the couch. Then Blake again bent over him, and as he did so he uttered a low exclamation of amazement, for now, for the first time, he saw the man's features plainly.

And the man who had been foully murdered at his very door was Captain Corner's Chinese cook.

THE SEVENTH CHAPTER.

Hong-Lo-Soo Smiles.

BLAKE sent Tinker out to get hold of a constable, while he himself phoned through to Scotland Yard and asked for Detective Inspector Thomas. He was fortunate enough to find the inspector in his office, and asked him, if possible, to come through to Baker Street at once. The inspector promised to do so, and just as Blake hung up the receiver Tinker appeared with a constable in tow.

The officer was from the near-by "beat," and in a few words the detective explained what had occurred. He also told him that Inspector Thomas was coming along, so there was nothing the constable could do until his superior arrived.

The inspector must have left immediately after hearing from Blake, for it seemed only a few minutes later that they heard the sound of a taxi outside, and then the bell rang. Tinker admitted the inspector, and when he had taken a look at the body on the couch he seated himself beside Blake's desk to take down the latter's statement.

In this Blake made no reference to the suspicions he had in his own mind. His theory was altogether too tenuous, so far, for him to commit himself to any definite hypothesis, but he did intimate that it might be possible for him, later on, to give the inspector a lead as to what line of inquiry might be worth while following; and knowing that Blake must have something in his mind, the inspector was content. Nor did Blake say that he and Tinker had already seen the dead man before. When the inspector had finished taking down Blake's statement he asked a few questions, and then reached for the phone.

"I'll get the body removed in the ambulance," he said. "It's a good thing this happened on your steps instead of on those of an ordinary citizen. There would have been a lovely howl. But I'm not surprised at all. We have lately been having a lot of trouble with Chinese here in London, as well as in Liverpool and Cardiff. There was a round-up in Cardiff the other day, and more than two hundred were roped in who had no papers and who were unregistered.

"They are slipping into the country at half a dozen points. And they are having their troubles in the United States as well. I see by the papers that there is a big tong war raging all the way from New York down through the New England States, and that hundreds of Chinks are fleeing inland. It is all the mess in China, and it will continue while things there are as they are."

He kept up his grumbling while he waited for his number, and then, when he got through, he asked for the ambulance to be sent on at once. They sat smoking and talking until it arrived, and it was with something of a sigh of relief that Blake finally saw the inspector take his departure, A little knot of people had collected at the appearance of the ambulance, but the constable soon shooed them away, and once more Blake and Tinker were left to carry out the purpose which Fate seemed to be persistently making a matter of considerable difficulty.

It was now nearly ten o'clock, and, as Blake did not wish to walk in on the merchant at that hour of the night without warning, he decided to telephone. He gave Hong-Lo-Soo's private number, and when a voice sounded at the other end of the wire he recognised it as that of the merchant himself.

Blake gave his name, and then said:

"I have had a cable from Hsui-fsi. I thought of calling on you to-night if convenient. I should have gone earlier, but have been detained. Will it be convenient?"

"Most assuredly, honourable friend," came the smooth accents of the Chinaman in flawless English. "I have been expecting to hear from you all day."

"Expecting to hear from me!" exclaimed Blake. "Did you receive a cable from Hsui-fsi?"

The merchant laughed softly. Then:

"No, honourable friend, I have not heard directly from the honourable Hsui-fsi for some time."

"Then why have you been expecting me?" asked Blake, puzzled.

"Come along, my friend, and I will tell you when you come," was the noncommittal answer; and, with another soft laugh, the merchant hung up.

On the way there Blake was puzzled over the dramatic and tragic incident that had occurred at his very door.

There was not the slightest doubt that the Celestial who had been murdered was Captain Corner's cook —the same man who had appeared so suddenly and mysteriously when Blake had been talking to the captain in the cabin the previous afternoon, who had waited on them at supper, and who had been standing on the back porch when they drove away in the morning.

The thing that intrigued him was how the man could have got to London so soon. And that was exactly what Tinker was thinking, for he voiced the question.

"I have been wondering that as well," was Blake's response. "As I figure it, my lad, he must have made his way into Brinscombe and caught the train there. I think the London train would pass through there somewhere about noon; and if he caught that he would reach London early this evening. Yes, that must be the explanation."

"It looks as if he had come up to see you, guv'nor," remarked Tinker.

"Yes, it does. And I am beginning to have the inkling of a suspicion why he wished to see me. He said something just before he died."

"What did he say, sir?"

"I cannot be sure —his words were choked with blood —but it sounded like, 'The Sacred Finger of the Daughter of Heaven.' "

"Gee! Is that the Empress' Little Finger again? I read what you had written in your notebook."

"Well, Tinker, it looks that way to me. In fact, my lad, I have a hunch that we have stumbled on to a first-class plot in connection with that business, and I have a further hunch that the red lacquered table has something to do with it. But here we are at Packer's Court. We shall see what Hong-Lo-Soo has to say."

Tinker drove into the dingy-looking court on which the big warehouses faced, and pulled up before a heavy wooden entrance door. As they stepped out the door swung open, and a Chinese youth stood bowing in the aperture.

"My honourable master expects the honourable guests," he said, and with that led them through the warehouse, which smelt pleasantly of Eastern spices, and through a door at the rear, which gave on to the staircase leading to Hong-Lo-Soo's private apartments at the back.

They mounted the staircase, and another heavy door at the top was opened. Then they passed through two outer ante-rooms, which were furnished in Chinese fashion with mats and bamboo furniture, and from the inner one along a corridor to another door. On this their guide tapped, and then opened it.

They entered, to find themselves in Hong-Lo-Soo's private

receiving-room —a most gorgeously and richly furnished room, in which both Blake and Tinker had often received the merchant's hospitality.

Hong-Lo-Soo was seated in a low chair beside a table, reading. He was dressed in full European evening-dress, and as they came in he rose and walked forward, with a smile of welcome. Then he led them towards a great divan at one end of the room, and no sooner were they seated than a boy entered bearing a tray on which reposed little eggshell teacups and a pot of fragrant Suchong tea. There was also a silver dish of Santok almonds and a box of yellow cigarettes. This the boy placed on a small tabourette, and Hong-Lo-Soo set about to do the honours himself. But before the boy had departed he snapped his fingers and said:

"Present my humble duties to the high and honourable lady, and my prayers that she will honour our unworthy company with her unapproachable presence."

The boy disappeared, and, although Blake was a little puzzled at the merchant's words —for he knew Hong-Lo-Soo did not have his wife in England —he, of course, made no remark. But a moment later, as the heavy yellow silk curtains were thrust aside and a soft, slurring footstep sounded, he noticed that Hong-Lo-Soo rose. He and Tinker also got to their feet and turned in the direction from which the sound came.

As he swung round Blake saw a wonderful vision of billowing, flowered silk coming towards them with the little, mincing step of the high-born Chinese lady whose feet have been bound in childhood. She was, even from Western standards, a very beautiful little creature, and would have roused the admiration of any man. But while he felt that all right, Blake was feeling something else much more acutely.

And that was sheer, dumbfounded amazement; for in the little lady who was mincing along like some lovely dream out of old China he recognised the same little creature who had visited him so mysteriously in his room at the farm in Devon the night before.

He managed to bow and give no sign, but as he caught sight of Hong-Lo-Soo's face he saw that the merchant was smiling enigmatically.

THE EIGHTH CHAPTER.

Which Explains a Lot.

BLAKE learned that the lady's name was Princess Yen-to. She seated herself on a small divan near the larger one, and Hong-Lo-Soo served her with one of the tiny cups of tea.

Then he served Blake and Tinker, and after taking one himself he turned and spoke a few rapid words in Chinese to the princess. Blake understood him to be asking her if he should do the talking, and she inclined her head in assent. Then the merchant seated himself facing Blake and said:

"Yes, I have been expecting you all day, honourable friend. The honourable princess arrived by train this evening, and came straight here. She telegraphed to me from a small town in the country, and I sent my car to meet her."

"From Brinscombe," murmured Blake, and the merchant nodded.

"She has told me about the lacquered table," went on Hong-Lo-Soo; "and, of course, you must have thought things very strange at that place last night. But I shall now explain."

Blake held up his hand.

"One moment, honourable friend!" he said. "Perhaps I can save you time. Am I correct in thinking that the red lacquered table which has caused so much anxiety to the honourable Princess Yen-to has something to do with the Sacred Finger of the Daughter of Heaven? Or, in other words, with what is known as the Empress' Little Finger?"

If Hong-Lo-Soo had surprised Blake by telling him that he had been expecting him all day, Blake certainly got square with his friend then, for the usual impassiveness of the Chinaman cracked in amazement as he stared at Blake.

"Honourable friend, it is so," he stammered. "But how did you know it?"

"Let us be brief," said Blake, with a smile and a glance towards the princess, who was looking at him with a curious expression. "Let us first deal with the Empress' Little Finger as I know the story —as I had it from the honourable Hsui-fsi.

"At the time of the revolution in China, in 1911, it is a fact, I believe, that the tomb of the late dowager-empress was opened by vandals, and one of the little fingers —the one on the left hand —was cut off, exactly for what reason it is not known. This meant terrible sacrilege among your race, Hong-Lo-Soo, and I believe it is a fact that the little finger has not been seen since.

"As time went on it became almost a legend. It was sought for everywhere, for it was said that the empress could not rest at peace among her ancestors until it was restored. But it was not known into whose hands it had fallen.

"Then, as the intrigues in China became more and more complex, it came to be believed that he who should be able to secure this relic —if I may use the term —would be in a position to strengthen the royalist party considerably, for if they were able to restore the finger by a well-advertised public ceremony, it would enable them to bring back the boy emperor, and, in the flood of reverence which the great majority of the Chinese have for the late empress, they would accept him, and clear out the numerous intriguing generals. Am I right?"

"Perfectly, honourable friend. Pray proceed."

"As I have said, the finger disappeared. I have no idea into whose hands it has fallen, but I have formed a theory, which I shall outline. This theory is that, in some way, it was secured by persons who were loyal to the person and memory of the late Empress. In the sack of the Sacred City in 1911, this person, or these persons, managed to put the finger in a place of safety, and, such care did they take to ensure that it should remain there until the right time to produce it that the secret was known to a very limited number of persons —probably not more than two or three.

"And, to make doubly sure, a very old Chinese ruse was resorted to in order, to doubly safeguard it. That ruse was a cryptogram, which was recorded in gold letters on the surface of a red-lacquered table, and the key-word of which was known only to those in the secret. The cryptogram was so complicated that some written record had to be made, for it would be impossible for anyone to carry the whole thing in his or her mind. That may or may not be right, but it is my theory. Then —"

"Wait, I pray you, honourable sir," broke in the princess, who was leaning, forward gazing at Blake as if he were some magician of old. "What you have said is just as it happened, but the reason why no one was allowed to carry the cryptogram in the mind was also because of the fear that the secret might be tortured out of them. If one did not know it, one could not reveal it."

"Thank you, honourable lady. That is another phase of the care of your honourable race for details, and reveals that they knew with whom they had to deal. I am gratified that my theory has been the correct one. And now, am I right in saying that in the flight from the palace these persons who knew the secret escaped, and managed to take the red-lacquered table with them?

"Am I also right in submitting that they made their escape through the good offices of one Captain Corner, a mariner who was plying on the China Coast at the time? And is it correct that, when he retired, Captain Corner brought some of those refugees with him to England, and that they have been in his house ever since?"

"True, true, true, honourable sir! At the time of the sack of the Sacred City I was a child. I escaped in the arms of my mother, who was second lady-in-waiting to the Empress during her lifetime. My mother brought the red-lacquered table with her, and the honourable Captain Corner took us under his care. We never dared return to China, but lived in Hong-Kong for some time, under the care of English people, and then my mother died.

"Captain Corner came to me and offered to care for me, and I came with him to this country. With us came my servant, who has been loyal and faithful. An explanation is due to you about last night, honourable sir. A man has been killed. Now that the Son of Heaven, the glorious Pi-Yu, has escaped from his enemies and is free, it is time that the Sacred Finger of the Daughter of Heaven should be given to him. so that he may return it to the tomb of his illustrious ancestor.

"There are many others who also seek the Sacred Finger. They are from every faction which struggles in China today. And last night some of those evil men came to the farm of the honourable Captain Corner. The honourable captain was not himself last night, and we did not know whether we could trust the honourable guest, or not. Therefore, the faithful San had to meet the evil men and deal with them. He drove them off, but one was killed.

"I had pleaded with the honourable captain to take back the table, but I could not tell even him what its secret was. He refused, for he said he had given his promise and must keep it. Then —then, honourable sir, I made direct appeal to you."

And here the little lady blushed violently.

"But still the honourable captain insisted that you should take the table with you, so there was nothing to do but follow you to London, and seek the aid of Hong-Lo-Soo, while I sent San to remind you of your promise. It was not San who attacked the honourable young sir last night.

"It was another servant, who wished to warn me that the evil men had got into the place, and to draw your attention while I reached safety. That is all, honourable sir; and from what the good and honourable Hong-Lo-Soo says I am now content, for I know you will give me back the table."

"Most certainly, princess," said Blake quickly. "The table is at my house, and is yours as soon as I can get it here. I think it would be safer with you, honourable friend, than anywhere else. From what Hsui-fsi says in his cable, I gather that there are many desperate men abroad seeking this table and the mystery it holds. In some way, they do know that it is the table that will yield up the secret of the Empress' Little Finger. But one thing I can't understand is why it was allowed to rest so long in that undefended place in Devon."

"Oh, honourable sir, that was the safest place for it!" broke in the princess. "No one would ever think of it being there, in full sight of anyone who might chance to enter."

And Blake had to acknowledge the subtlety and soundness of her strategy.

Then he looked at the merchant.

"Can you arrange to come round with us to-night?" he asked. "If you will do so, we shall all come back and bring the lacquered table with us, and then the princess can sleep content. And later on, perhaps, she will tell me just where the Sacred Finger is to be found."

"I will tell the honourable sir now," she said. "It lies at the bottom of the Lake of Four Moons in the Imperial Gardens in the Sacred City. The secret of the table tells the exact spot, and he who knows that secret may go and bring up the box in which the Sacred Finger was placed. And the honourable Hong-Lo-Soo has promised that this will be done, so that when the glorious Son of Heaven comes to this country I may return to him the sacred relic of his illustrious ancestor."

Blake nodded at the simplicity of it all, and yet it was the very simplicity which had been its great safety. He thought then that the mother of the Princess Yen-to must have been a very shrewd Chinese lady to think out the scheme; and, as a matter of fact, he was dead right, for the late princess, who had been second lady-in-waiting to the Empress, had been one of the powers behind the throne at the Imperial Court.

But Blake had conveyed something else to Hong-Lo-Soo in his glance, and the Chinaman knew that he had something to say to him privately. So he rose and suggested that the princess should not fatigue herself further, but should retire while they went to get the red-lacquered table. She accepted this suggestion, and, after several formal little curtseys, passed behind the curtains. No sooner was she gone than Blake said:

"I think we had better go along at once. What I wanted to tell you, honourable friend, was that her servant, San, was murdered on my doorstep this evening, and I am wondering what move the enemy may make next."

In one of Sexton Blake's chairs sat Mrs. Bardell, bound hand and foot, and gagged. She was obviously suffering considerable pain from the brutal way the gag had been jammed into her mouth. (*Page* 22.)

Turning the Tables.

AS Tinker drew into the kerb in front of their own house, he noticed a light against the drawn blinds of the consulting-room and turned round.

"I say, guv'nor." he remarked,— "did you leave the consulting-room light on when we came out?"

"No. I did nothing to the switch. I thought you turned it out."

"Well, that is what I thought —could have sworn I did. Perhaps Mrs. Bardell is in there."

And she was, but in a very different way from what Tinker thought.

They all got out and mounted the steps. Tinker took out his key and opened the door, and, with a word of apology to Hong-Lo-Soo, Blake led the way along to the consulting-room.

Tinker closed the door and came along last.

He was still some little distance down the corridor when Blake opened the door, and then he heard his master utter a sharp exclamation as he disappeared into the room. Hong-Lo-Soo also said something as he reached the threshold, and a second or so later, when he, too, got there, Tinker was almost profane. And little wonder, for in one of Blake's saddlebag chairs was Mrs. Bardell, bound hand and foot and gagged, and obviously suffering considerable pain from the brutal way in which the gag had been jammed in her mouth.

Blake, full of concern, was already bending over her, loosening the gag, and Tinker, with a red mist of anger before his eyes, was fumbling at her bonds. He had a great feeling of tenderness in him for Mrs. Bardell, for she had been almost a mother to him in the days when he had been just a little London street waif, and in that moment there was sheer lust to kill those who had manhandled her in such fashion.

As soon as they got her free, Tinker, at a word from Blake, ran along to the dining-room and got the brandy decanter. Blake poured some of the spirit between Mrs. Bardell's lips, and she sat up, gasping. Blake did not urge her to speak, but, needless to say, he was more than anxious to know what had happened. And just then Tinker noticed that the red-lacquered table was no longer where it had been when they left for Hong-Lo-Soo's.

"The table!" he gasped. "It's gone!"

Blake swung round like a shot and saw that what the lad said was a fact. Then he turned back to Mrs. Bardell, who was trying to speak.

"Yes," she was saying huskily, "them yeller fiends came in and took it. I heard a ring at the bell, and went to the door. There they were a-standing, three of 'em, and they pushed me back into the house before I could slam the door in their yeller faces. They choked me and brought me in here and tied me up like what you found me. Then they took the table and went."

"Which way did they go?" asked Blake quickly. "By the front door?"

"No. Along the passage towards the laboratory."

Tinker made a jump for the door leading to that passage and opened it. He stood listening, and then he turned sharply.

"By thunder, I don't think they have got out yet," he whispered. "I'm going after them."

He ran to his desk and jerked out a drawer, taking up the heavier of two pistols which lay there. Blake was busy doing the same at his desk, and Hong-Lo-Soo motioned to Tinker to give him the extra gun. Then, leaving Mrs. Bardell for the moment, they ran on their toes along the passage.

Tinker was in the lead, and as he wrenched open the door of the laboratory his finger automatically found the light-switch. The next second the room was flooded in brilliance, and the lad gave a cry as he saw two figures standing just inside the window in the very act of passing the lacquered table out to someone outside.

They were Chinese, as Mrs. Bardell had said, and both men whirled with jabbered oaths as the light flashed on. The precious table dropped with a crash, and both men clawed for their weapons. But Tinker's gun was already beginning to spit, and sharp on that Blake's pistol crashed out, followed in the same second by Hong-Lo-Soo's.

Blake and Tinker, following their usual custom, had been shooting low, but Hong-Lo-Soo, who knew no such creed where those of an enemy tong were concerned, had shot to kill, and if he had been more familiar with the balance of Tinker's lighter weapon he would have drilled the man outside the window clean between the eyes. As it was his bullet caught him just at the top of the forehead and sent him down before he could get his gun over the sill. Blake's bullet caught the man on the right in the thigh, and Tinker made a hit in the body. Tinker's man also passed out of the fight, but Blake's man, wounded though he was, managed to get his weapon out, and began shooting in frenzied fashion.

The bullets crashed into the floor and wall all about them, and it was a miracle of bad shooting, or, rather, of a shaky hand due to his wound, that he did not get one of them. But Blake cut him short with a bullet in his right arm, and then they rushed.

In five minutes it was all over, and while Blake and Hong-Lo-Soo gave first-aid treatment to the wounds, Tinker went along to try and get through to Inspector Thomas, whom he was lucky enough to find was still engaged on the case which Blake had been the means of giving him earlier in the evening.

Needless to say, the inspector was more than pleased at the haul he was able to make, for Scotland Yard had received special information about this new gang of Chinese which had come to England, and in view of the possibility of the arrival of Pu-Yi, the boy emperor, they were straining every nerve to make a clean sweep of all the doubtful ones before his arrival. And in this trio they had the actual ringleaders of the plot, though, of course, Scotland Yard didn't know the whole truth of that until Blake gave them the particulars.

It was early in the morning when the Grey Panther once more took its way to Packer's Court, and once more the red-lacquered table reposed in the tonneau. Once it was inside the warehouse Blake heaved a sigh of relief, for now the thing was off his hands, and he had been able to keep his word to the Princess Yen-to. He and Tinker remained long enough to drink another cup of tea with Hong-Lo-Soo; then they drove back to Baker Street, only too glad at the prospect of sleep at last, although they were chiefly anxious to know that Mrs. Bardell was all right.

They talked things over in the consulting-room after she had assured them that she was feeling better and had taken herself to bed. Tinker, as usual, had some point to raise, and this time it was a curiosity to know what the Empress' Little Finger was like.

Blake smiled as he blew a smoke-ring ceilingwards.

"We shall possibly get a chance to have a look at it, my lad. But I shall venture the opinion that when we do we shall see just a shrivelled bit of mummified flesh on the bone, with a fingernail three inches long, and this encased in a gold shield which would be worn during life as a protection. In the case of a person like the late Dowager Empress of China we shall probably find that the gold shield is gem-studded. You must have seen something of the sort China."

"Sure, I did. I remember now, guv'nor. And will the princess hand it over to the young emperor?"

"That, I take it, is her intention when Hong-Lo-Soo's agent brings it back from where it now lies. But what will become of it then no one can say. With that in his possession, Pi-Yu can return to the tomb of his illustrious ancestor, and by placing it back in the tomb break the curse which is supposed to have been hanging over the Imperial Family ever since it was stolen.

"But that is up to him. It will need a very wise head to find a path to safety and power through the intriguing hordes who are making a cockpit out of China to-day. And now come on, my lad. To bed! To-morrow we must send a cable to Sir Gordon, and I suppose Captain Corner will turn up. I think we have a slight surprise to give the old man about his lacquered table."

THE END.
[20200 WORDS]

NEWCOMERS PLEASE NOTE

—this feature, the U. J. Detective Supplement normally consists of EIGHT pages, so arranged that they can be detached easily and bound up into volume form at the end of each years issues.

In view of the extra long serial instalment and important competition announcements this week, however, the usual eight pages are temporarily reduced to four.

The full number will be reverted to immediately, when restrictions of space no longer prevent their inclusion.

Regular "U. J." readers realise this feature is unique —no other paper has anything like it.

The Supplement was missing from my copy of this issue.../drf

The BEGINNING of our GREAT SERIAL

Captain Blood

by Rafael Sabatini

(*The ORIGINAL Story of the great Vitagraph Film.*)

Now starting the serial **Captain Blood** *by Rafael Sabatini*
(The ORIGINAL Story of the great Vitagraph Film.)

CHAPTER ONE.

The Messenger.

PETER BLOOD, bachelor of medicine and several other things besides, smoked a pipe and tended the geraniums boxed on the sill of his window above Water Lane in the town of Bridgewater.

Sternly disapproving eyes considered him from a window opposite, but went disregarded. Mr. Blood's attention was divided between his task and the stream of humanity in the narrow street below; a stream which poured for the second time that day in the direction of Castle Field, where, earlier, in the afternoon, Ferguson, the Duke's chaplain, had preached a sermon containing more treason than divinity.

These straggling, excited groups were mainly composed of men with green boughs in their hats and the most ludicrous of weapons in their hands. Some, it is true, shouldered fowling-pieces, and here and there a sword was brandished; but more of them were armed with clubs, and most of them trailed the mammoth pikes fashioned out of scythes, as formidable to the eye as they were clumsy to the hand.

There were weavers, brewers, carpenters, smiths, masons, bricklayers, cobblers, and representatives of every other of the trades of peace among these improvised men of war. Bridgewater, like Taunton, had yielded so generously of its manhood to the service of the illegitimate Duke that for any to abstain whose age and strength admitted of his bearing arms was to brand himself a coward or a Papist.

Yet Peter Blood, who was not only able to bear arms and skilled in their use, who was certainly no coward, and a Papist only when it suited him, tended his geraniums and smoked his pipe on that warm July evening as indifferently as if nothing were afoot. One other thing he did. He flung after those war-fevered enthusiasts a line of Horace —a poet for whose work he had early conceived an inordinate affection.

"Quo, quo, scelesti, ruitis?"

And now perhaps you guess why the hot, intrepid blood inherited from the roving sires of his Somersetshire mother remained cool amidst all this frenzied heat of rebellion; why the turbulent spirit which had forced them once from the sedate academical bonds his father would have imposed upon him, would now remain quiet in the very midst of turbulence.

You realise how he regarded these men who were rallying to the banners of liberty —the banners woven by the virgins of Taunton, the girls from the seminaries of Miss Blake and Mrs. Musgrove, who — as the ballad runs —had ripped open their silk petticoats to make colours for King Monmouth's army. That Latin line contemptuously flung after them as they clattered down the cobbled street reveals his mind. To him they were fools rushing in wicked frenzy upon their ruin.

You see, he knew too much about this fellow Monmouth to be deceived by the legend of legitimacy, on the strength of which this standard of rebellion had been raised.

He had read the absurd proclamation posted at the Cross at Bridgewater —as it had been posted at Taunton and else-where — setting forth that upon the decease of our Sovereign Lord Charles the Second, the right of succession to the Crown of England, Scotland, France, and Ireland with the dominions and territories thereunto belonging, did legally descend and devolve upon the most illustrious and high-born Prince James, Duke of Monmouth, and heir-apparent to the said King Charles the Second.

It had moved him to laughter, as had the further announcement that "James Duke of York did first cause the said late King to be poisoned, and immediately thereupon did usurp and invade the Crown."

He knew not which was the greater lie. For Mr. Blood had spent a third of his life in the Netherlands, where this same James Scott — who now proclaimed himself James the Second, by the Grace of God, King, et cetera — first saw the light some six-and-thirty years ago, and he was acquainted with the story current there of the fellow's real paternity. Far from being legitimate — by virtue of a pretended secret marriage between Charles Stuart and Lucy Walter — it was possible that this Monmouth who now proclaimed himself King of England was not even the illegitimate child of the late sovereign.

What but ruin and disaster could be the end of this grotesque pretension? How could it be hoped that England should ever swallow such a Perkin? And it was on his behalf, to uphold his fantastic claim, that these West Country clods, led by a few armigerous Whigs, had been seduced into rebellion!

"Quo, quo, scelesti, ruitis?"

He laughed and sighed in one; but the laugh dominated the sigh, for Mr. Blood was unsympathetic, as are most self-sufficient men; and he was very self-sufficient — adversity had taught him so to be.

A more tender-hearted man, possessing his vision and his knowledge, might have found cause for tears, in the contemplation of these ardent, simple non-conformist sheep going forth to the shambles — escorted to the rallying ground on Castle Field by wives and daughters, sweethearts, and mothers, sustained by the delusion that they were to take the field in defence of Right, of Liberty, and of Religion.

For he knew, as all Bridgewater knew and had known now for some hours, that it was Monmouth's intention to deliver battle that same night. The Duke was to lead a surprise attack upon the Royalist army under Feversham that was now encamped on Sedgemoor.

Mr. Blood thought it very probable that Lord Feversham was equally well-informed, and if in this assumption he was wrong, at least he was justified of it. He was not to suppose the Royalist commander so indifferently skilled in the trade he followed.

Mr. Blood knocked the ashes from his pipe and drew back to close his window. As he did so, his glance travelling straight across the street met at last the glance of those hostile eyes that watched him.

There were two pairs, and they belonged to the Misses Pitt, two amiable, sentimental maiden ladies who yielded to none in Bridgewater in their worship of the handsome Monmouth.

Mr. Blood smiled and inclined his head, for he was on friendly terms with these ladies, one of whom, indeed, had been for a little while his patient.

But there was no response to his greeting. Instead, the eyes gave him back a stare of cold disdain. The smile on his thin lips grew a little broader, a little less pleasant. He understood the reason of that hostility, which had been daily growing in this past week since Monmouth had come to turn the brain of women of all ages.

The Misses Pitt, he apprehended, contemned him that he, a young and vigorous man, of a military training which might now be valuable to the cause, should stand aloof, that he should placidly smoke his pipe and tend his geraniums on this evening of all evenings when men of spirit were rallying to the Protestant Champion, offering their blood to place him on the throne where he belonged.

If Mr. Blood had condescended to debate the matter with these ladies, he might have urged that having had his fill of wandering and adventuring, he was now embarked upon the career for which he had been originally intended and for which his studies had equipped him; that he was a man of medicine and not of war; a healer, not a slayer. But they would have answered him, he knew, that in such a cause it behoved every man who deemed himself a man to take up arms.

They would have pointed out that their own nephew Jeremiah, who was by trade a sailor, the master of a ship —which by an ill-chance for that young man had come to anchor at this season in Bridgewater Bay —had quitted the helm to snatch up a musket in defence of Right.

But Mr. Blood was not of those who argue. As I have said, he was a self-sufficient man.

He closed the window, drew the curtains, and turned to the pleasant, candle-lighted room, and the table on which Mrs. Barlow, his housekeeper, was in the very act of spreading supper. To her, however, he spoke aloud his thought.

"It's out of favour I am with the vinegary virgins over the way!"

He had a pleasant, vibrant voice, whose metallic ring was softened and muted by the Irish accent which in all his wanderings he had never lost. It was a voice that could woo seductively and caressingly, or command in such a way as to compel obedience. Indeed, the man's whole nature was in that voice of his.

For the rest of him, he was tall and spare, swarthy of tint as a gipsy, with eyes that were startlingly blue in that dark face and under those level black brows. In their glance those eyes, flanking a high-bridged, intrepid nose, were of singular penetration, and of a steady haughtiness that went well with his firm lips.

Though dressed in black as became his calling, yet it was with an elegance derived from the love of clothes that is peculiar to the adventurer he had been, rather than to the staid medicus he now was.

His coat was of fine camlet, and it was laced with silver; there were ruffles of Mechlin at his wrists and a Mechlin cravat encased his throat. His great black periwig was as sedulously curled as any at Whitehall.

Seeing him thus, and perceiving his real nature, which was plain upon him, you might have been tempted to speculate how long such a man would be content to lie by this little backwater of the world into which chance had swept him some six months ago; how long he would continue to pursue the trade for which he had qualified himself before he had begun to live.

Difficult of belief though it may be when you know his history, previous and subsequent, yet it is possible that but for the trick that Fate was about to play him, he might have continued this peaceful existence, settling down completely to the life of a doctor in this Somersetshire haven. It is possible, but not probable.

He was the son of an Irish medieus, by a Somersetshire lady in whose veins ran the rover blood of the Frobishers, which may account for a certain wildness that had early manifested itself in his disposition. This wildness had profoundly alarmed his father, who for an Irishman was of a singularly peace-loving nature. He had early resolved that the boy should follow his own honourable profession, and Peter Blood being quick to learn and oddly greedy of knowledge, had satisfied his parent by receiving at the age of twenty the degree of bacca-laureus medicinae at Trinity College, Dublin.

His father survived that satisfaction by three months only. His mother had then been dead some years already. Thus Peter Blood came into an inheritance of some few hundred pounds, with which he had set out to see the world and give for a season a free rein to that restless spirit by which he was imbued.

A set of curious chances led him to take service with the Dutch, then at war with France; and a predilection for the sea made him elect that this service should be upon that element. He had the advantage of a commission under the famous de Ruyter, and fought in the Mediterranean engagement in which that great Dutch admiral lost his life.

After the Peace of Nimeguen his movements are obscure. But we know that he spent two years in a Spanish prison, though we do not know how he contrived to get there. It may be clue to this that upon his release he took his sword to France, and saw service with the French in their warring upon the Spanish Netherlands.

Having reached, at last, the age of thirty-two, his appetite for adventure surfeited, his health having grown indifferent as the result of a neglected wound, he was suddenly overwhelmed by homesickness. He took ship from Nantes with intent to cross to Ireland.

But the vessel being driven by stress of weather into Bridgewater Bay, and Blood's health having grown worse during the voyage, he decided to go ashore there, additionally urged to it by the fact that it was his mother's native soil.

Thus in January of that year 1685 he had come to Bridgewater, possessor of a fortune that was approximately the same as that with which he had originally set out from Dublin eleven years ago.

Because he liked the place, in which his health was rapidly restored to him, and because he conceived that he had passed through adventures enough for a man's lifetime, he determined to settle there, and take up at last the profession of medicine from which he had, with so little profit, broken away.

That is all his story, or so much of it as matters up to that night, six months later, when the battle of Sedgemoor was fought.

Deeming the impending action no affair of his, as indeed it was not, and indifferent to the activity with which Bridgewater was that night agog, Mr. Blood closed his ears to the sounds of it and went early to bed. He was peacefully asleep long before eleven o'clock, at which hour, as you know, Monmouth rode out with his rebel host along the Bristol Road, circuitously to avoid the marshland that lay directly between himself and the Royal Army.

You also know that his numerical advantage —possibly counterbalanced by the greater steadiness of the regular troops on the other side —and the advantages he derived from falling by surprise upon an army that was more or less asleep, were all lost to him by blundering and bad leadership before ever he was at grips with Feversham.

The armies came into collision in the neighbourhood of two o'clock in the morning. Mr. Blood slept undisturbed through the distant boom of cannon. Not until four o'clock, when the sun was rising to dispel the last wisps of mist over that stricken field of battle, did he awaken from his tranquil slumbers.

He sat up in bed, rubbed the sleep from his eyes, and collected himself. Blows were thundering upon the door of his house, and a voice was calling incoherently. This was the noise that had aroused him. Conceiving that he had to do with some urgent case, he reached for bedgown and slippers, to go below.

On the landing he almost collided with Mrs. Barlow, new-risen and unsightly, in a state of panic. He quieted her duckings with a word of reassurance, and went himself to open.

There in slanting golden light of the new-risen sun stood a breathless, wildeyed man and a steaming horse. Smothered in dust and grime, his clothes in disarray, the left sleeve of his doublet hanging in rags, this young man opened his lips to speak, yet for a long moment remained speechless.

In that moment Mr. Blood recognised him for the young shipmaster, Jeremiah Pitt, the nephew of the maiden ladies opposite, one who had been drawn by the general enthusiasm into the vortex of that rebellion. The street was rousing, awakened by the sailor's noisy advent; doors were opening, and lattices were being unlatched for the protrusion of anxious, inquisitive heads.

"Take your time, now," said Mr. Blood. "I never knew speed made by overhaste."

But the wild-eyed lad paid no heed to the admonition. He plunged, headlong, into speech, gasping, breathless. "It is Lord Gildoy," he panted, "He is sore wounded —at Oglethorpe's Farm by the river. I bore him thither, and —and he sent me for you. Come away! Come away!"

He would have clutched the doctor, and hauled him forth by force in bedgown and slippers as he was. But the doctor eluded that too eager hand.

"To be sure, I'll come," said he. He was distressed. Gildoy had been a very friendly, generous patron to him since his settling in these parts. And Mr. Blood was eager enough to do what he now could to discharge the debt, grieved that the occasion should have arisen, and in such a manner —for he knew quite well that the rash young nobleman had been an active agent of the Duke's. "To be sure, I'll come. But first give me leave to get some clothes and other things that I may need."

"There's no time to lose."

"Be easy now. I'll lose none. I tell ye again, ye'll go quickest by going leisurely. Come in —take a chair —"

He threw open the door of a parlour.

Young Pitt waved aside the invitation.

"I'll wait here. Make haste, in God's name."

Mr. Blood went off to dress and to fetch a case of instruments.

Questions concerning the precise nature of Lord Gildoy's hurt could wait until they were on their way. Whilst he pulled on his boots he gave Mrs. Barlow instructions for the day. which included the matter of a dinner he was not destined to eat.

When at last he went forth again, Mrs. Barlow clucking after him like a disgruntled fowl, he found young Pitt smothered in a crowd of scared, half-dressed townsfolk —mostly women —who had come hastening for news of how the battle had sped. The news he gave them was to be read in the lamentations with which they disturbed the morning air.

At sight of the doctor, dressed and booted, the case of instruments tucked under his arm, the messenger disengaged himself from those who pressed about, shook off his weariness and the two tearful aunts, that clung most closely, and, seizing the bridle of his horse, he climbed to the saddle.

"Come along, sir!" he cried. "Mount quickly. I'll get up behind ye."

Mr. Blood, without wasting words, did as he was bidden. He touched the horse with his heels. The little crowd gave way, and thus, on that doubly-laden horse, with his companion clinging to his belt, Peter Blood set out upon his Odyssey. For this Pitt, in whom he beheld no more than the messenger of a wounded rebel gentleman, was indeed the very messenger of Fate.

RAFAEL SABATINI!—The famous author of " Captain Blood."

READ the STORY—
SEE the FILM !

Don't neglect this unique opportunity of seeing a good story as well as reading it.
Turn to page 24, and see whether the Vitagraph film of "Captain Blood" is showing in your district yet.

Peter Blood touched the horse with his heels, and, with Pitt behind him, set out. Thus, on that doubly-laden horse, he set out on his Odyssey. *(Page 4.)*
[*Picture from the Vitagraph Film*

CHAPTER TWO.

Kirke's Dragoons.

OGLETHORPE'S Farm stood a mile or so to the south of Bridgewater on the right bank of the river. It was a straggling Tudor building showing grey above the ivy that clothed its lower parts. Approaching it now, through the fragrant orchards amid which it seemed to drowse in Arcadian peace beside the waters of the Parrett, sparkling in the morning sunlight, Mr. Blood might have had a difficulty in believing it part of a world tormented by strife and bloodshed.

On the bridge, as they had been riding out of Bridgewater, they had met a vanguard of fugitives from the field of battle, weary, broken men, many of them wounded, all of them terror-stricken, staggering in speedless haste with the last remnants of their strength into the shelter which it was their vain illusion the town would afford them.

Eyes glazed with lassitude and fear looked up piteously out of haggard faces at Mr. Blood and his companion as they rode forth, hoarse voice cried a warning that merciless pursuit was not far behind. Undeterred, however, young Pitt rode amain along the dusty road by which these poor fugitives from that swift rout on Sedgemoor came flocking in ever-increasing numbers.

Presently he swung aside, and quitting the road took to a pathway that crossed the dewy meadowlands. Even here they met odd groups of these human derelicts, who were scattering in all directions, looking fearfully behind them as they came through the long grass, expecting at every moment to see the red coats of the dragoons.

But as Pitt's direction was a southward one, bringing them ever nearer to Feversham's headquarters, they were presently clear of that human flotsam and jetsam of the battle, and riding through the peaceful orchards heavy with the ripening fruit that was soon to make its annual yield of cider.

At last they alighted on the kidney stones of the courtyard, and Baynes, the master of the homestead, grave of countenance and flustered of manner, gave them welcome.

In the spacious, stone-flagged hall, the doctor found Lord Gildoy —a very tall and dark young gentleman, prominent of chin and nose —stretched on a cane day-bed under one of the tall mullioned windows, in the care of Mrs. Baynes and her comely daughter. His cheeks were leaden-hued, his eyes closed, and from his blue lips came with each laboured breath a faint moaning noise.

Mr. Blood stood for a moment silently considering his patient. He deplored that a youth with such bright hopes in life as Lord Gildoy's should have risked all, perhaps existence itself, to forward the ambition of a worthless adventurer. Because he had liked and honoured this brave lad he paid his case the tribute of a sigh. Then he knelt to his task, ripped away doublet and underwear to lay bare his lordship's mangled side, and called for water and linen and what else he needed for his work.

He was still intent upon it a half-hour later when the dragoons invaded the homestead. The clatter of hoofs and hoarse shouts that heralded their approach disturbed him not at all. For one thing, he was not easily disturbed; for another, his task absorbed him.

But his lordship, who had now recovered consciousness, showed considerable alarm, and the battle-stained Jeremy Pitt sped to cover in a clothes'-press. Baynes was uneasy, and his wife and daughter trembled. Mr. Blood reassured them.

"Why, what's to Fear?" he said. "It's a Christian country, this; and Christian men do not make war upon the wounded, nor upon those who harbour them." He still had, you see, illusions about Christians. He held a glass of cordial, prepared under his directions, to his lordship's lips. "Give your mind peace, my lord. The worst is done."

And then they came rattling and clanking into the stone-flagged hall —a round dozen jack-booted, lobster-coated troopers of the Tangier Regiment, led by a sturdy black-browed fellow with a deal of gold lace about the breast of his coat.

Baynes stood his ground, his attitude half-defiant, whilst his wife and daughter shrank away in renewed fear. Mr. Blood, at the head of the day-bed, looked over his shoulder to take stock of the invaders.

The officer barked an order, which brought his men to an attentive halt, then swaggered forward, his gloved hand bearing down the pummel of his sword, his spurs jingling musically as he moved. He announced his authority to the yeoman.

"I am Captain Hobart, of Colonel Kirke's dragoons. What rebels do you harbour?"

The yeoman took alarm at that ferocious truculence. It expressed itself in his trembling voice.

"I —I am no harbourer of rebels, sir. This wounded gentleman —"

"I can see for myself." The captain stamped forward to the day-bed. and scowled down upon the grey-faced sufferer. "No need to ask how he came in this state and by his wounds. A damned rebel, and that's enough for me." He flung a command at his dragoons. "Out with him, my lads!"

Mr. Blood got between the day-bed and the troopers.

"In the name of humanity, sir!" said he, on a note of anger. "'This is England, not Tangiers. The gentleman is in sore case. He may not be moved without peril to his life."

Captain Hobart was amused.

"Oh, I am to be tender of the lives of these rebels! Odds blood! Do you think it's to benefit his health we're taking him? There's gallows being planted along the road from Weston to Bridgewater, and he'll serve for one of them as well as another. Colonel Kirke'll learn these nonconforming oafs something they'll not forget in generations."

"You're hanging men without trial? Faith then, it's mistaken I am. We're in Tangiers after all, it seems, where your regiment belongs."

The captain considered him with a kindling eye. He looked him over from the soles of his riding-boots to the crown of his periwig. He noted the spare active frame, the arrogant poise of the head, the air of authority that invested Mr. Blood, and soldier recognised soldier. The captain's eyes narrowed. Recognition went further.

"Who may you be?" he exploded.

"My name is Blood, sir —Peter Blood, at your service."

"Ay, ay! Codso! That's the name. You were in French service once, were you not?"

If Mr. Blood was surprised he did not betray it.

"I was."

"Then I remember you —five years ago, or more, you were in Tangiers."

"That is so. I knew your colonel."

"Faith, you may be renewing the acquaintance." The captain laughed unpleasantly. "What brings you here, sir?"

"This wounded gentleman. I was fetched to attend him. I am a

66

medicus."

"A doctor —you?"

Scorn of that lie —as he conceived it —rang in the heavy, hectoring voice.

"Medicime baccalaureus," said Mr. Blood.

"Don't fling your French at me, man!" snapped Hobart. "Speak English!"

Mr. Blood's smile annoyed him.

"I am a physician practising my calling in the town of Bridgewater."

The captain sneered.

"Which you reached by way of Lyme Regis in the following of your Duke."

It was Mr. Blood's turn to sneer.

"If your wit were as big as your voice, my dear, it's the great man you'd be by this."

For a moment the dragoon was speechless. The colour deepened in his face.

"You may find me great enough to hang you."

"Faith, yes. Ye've the look and the manners of a hangman. But if you practise your trade on my patient here, you may be putting a rope round your own neck. He's not the kind you may string up and no questions asked. He has the right to trial, and the right to trial by his peers."

"By his peers?"

The captain was taken aback by these three words, which Mr. Blood had stressed.

"Sure now, any but a fool or a savage would have asked his name before ordering him to the gallows. The gentleman is my Lord Gildoy."

And then his lordship spoke for himself, in a weak voice:

"I make no concealment of my association with the Duke of Monmouth. I'll take the consequences. But if you please, I'll take them after trial —by my peers as the doctor has said."

The feeble voice, ceased, and was followed by a moment's silence. As is common in many blustering men, there was a deal of timidity deep down in Hobart. The announcement of his lordship's rank had touched those depths. A servile upstart, he stood in awe of titles. And he stood in awe of his colonel. Percy Kirke was not lenient with blunderers.

By a gesture he checked his men. He must consider Mr. Blood, observing his pause, added further matter for his consideration.

"Ye'll be remembering, captain, that Lord Gildoy will have friends and relatives on the Tory side, who'll have something to say to Colonel Kirke if his lordship should be handled like a common felon. You'll go warily, captain, or, as I've said, it's a halter for your neck ye'll be weaving this morning."

Captain Hobart swept the warning aside with a bluster of contempt, but he acted upon it none the less.

"Take up the day-bed," said he, "and convey him on that to Bridgewater. Lodge him in the gaol until I take order about him."

"He may not survive the journey," Blood remonstrated. "He's in no case to be moved."

"So much the worse for him. My affair is to round up rebels."

He confirmed his order by a gesture. Two of his men took up the day-bed, and swung to depart with it. Gildoy made a feeble effort to put forth a hand towards Mr. Blood.

"Sir," he said, "you leave me in your debt. If I live I shall study how to discharge it."

Mr. Blood bowed for answer, then to the men. "Bear him steadily," he commanded. "His life depends on it."

As his lordship was carried out, the captain became brisk. He turned upon the yeoman.

"What other cursed rebels do you harbour?"

"None other, sir. His lordship —"

"We've dealt with his lordship for the present. We'll deal with you in a moment when we've searched your house. And, by God, if you've lied to me —"

He broke off, snarling to give an order. Four of his dragoons went out. In a moment they were heard moving noisily in the adjacent room. Meanwhile, the captain was questing about the hall, sounding the wainscoting with the butt of a pistol.

Mr. Blood saw no profit in lingering.

"By your leave, it's a very good-day I'll be wishing you," said he.

"By my leave you'll remain awhile," the captain ordered him.

Mr. Blood shrugged, and sat down.

"You're tiresome," he said. "I wonder your colonel hasn't

discovered it yet."

But the captain did not heed him. He was stooping to pick up a soiled and dusty hat in which there was pinned a little bunch of oak leaves. It had been lying near the clothes' press in which the unfortunate Pitt had taken refuge. The captain smiled malevolently. His eyes raked the room, resting first sardonically on the yeoman, then on the two women in the background, and finally on Mr. Blood, who sat with one leg thrown over the other in an attitude of indifference that was far from reflecting his mind.

Then the captain stepped to the press, and pulled open one of the wings of its massive oaken door. He took the huddled inmate by the collar of his doublet, and lugged him out into the open.

"And who the devil's this?" quoth he. "Another nobleman?"

Mr. Blood had a vision of those gallows of which Captain Hobart had spoken, and of this unfortunate young shipmaster going to adorn one of them, strung up without trial, in the place of the other victim of whom the captain had been cheated. On the spot he invented not only a title but a whole family for the young rebel.

"Faith, ye've said it, captain! This is Viscount Pitt, first cousin to Sir Thomas Vernon, who's married to that slut, Moll Kirke, sister to your own colonel and sometime lady-in-waiting upon King James' queen."

Both the captain and his prisoner gasped. But whereas thereafter young Pitt discreetly held his peace, the captain rapped out a nasty oath. He considered his prisoner again.

"He's lying, is he not?" he demanded, seizing the lad by the shoulder and glaring into his face. "He's rallying me, by Heaven!"

"If ye believe that," said Blood, "hang him, and see what happens to you!"

The dragoon glared at the doctor and then at his prisoner.

"Pah!" He thrust the lad into the hands of his men. "Fetch him along to Bridgewater, and make fast that fellow also," He pointed to Baynes. "We'll show him what it means to harbour and comfort rebels."

There was a moment of confusion. Baynes struggled in the grip of the trappers, protesting vehemently. The terrified women screamed until silenced by a greater terror. The captain strode across to them. He took the girl by the shoulders. She was a pretty, golden-headed creature, with soft blue eyes that looked up entreatingly, piteously into the face of the dragoon. He leered upon her, his eyes aglow, took her chin in his hand, and set her shuddering by his brutal kiss.

"It's an earnest," he said, smiling grimly. "Let that quiet you, little rebel, till I've done with these rogues."

And he swung away again, leaving her faint and trembling in the arms of her anguished mother. His men stood, grinning, awaiting orders, the two prisoners now fast pinioned.

"Take them away. Let Cornet Drake have charge of them." His smouldering eye again sought the cowering girl. "I'll stay awhile —to search out this place. There may be other rebels hidden here." As an afterthought he added: "And take this fellow with you." He pointed to Mr. Blood, "Bestir!"

Mr. Blood started out of his musings. He had been considering that in his case of instruments there was a lancet with which he might perform on Captain Hobart a beneficial operation. Beneficial, that is, to humanity. In any case, the dragoon was obviously plethoric, and would be better for a blood-letting. The difficulty lay in making the opportunity. He was beginning to wonder if he could lure the captain aside with some tale o' hidden treasure, when this untimely interruption set a term to that interesting speculation.

He sought to temporise.

"Faith, it will suit me very well!" said he. "For Bridgewater is my destination, and but that ye detained me I'd have been on my way thither now."

"Your destination there will be the gaol."

"Ah, bah! Ye're surely joking."

"There's a gallows for you if you prefer it. It's merely a question of now or later."

Rude hands seized Mr. Blood, and that precious lancet was in the case on the table out of reach. He twisted out of the grip of the troopers, for he was strong and agile; but they closed with him again immediately, and bore him down. Pinning him to the ground, they tied his wrists behind his back, then roughly pulled him to his feet again.

"Take him away!" said Hobart shortly, and turned to issue his orders to the other waiting dragoons. "Go search the house from attic to cellar, then report to me here."

The soldiers trailed out by the door leading to the interior. Mr. Blood was thrust by his guards into the courtyard, where Pitt and

Baynes already waited. From the threshold of the hall he looked back at Captain Hobart, and his sapphire eyes were blazing. On his lips trembled a threat of what he would do to Hobart if he should happen to survive this business.

Betimes he remembered that to utter it were probably to extinguish his chance of living to execute it. For to-day the King's men were masters in the West, and the West was regarded as enemy country, to be subjected to the worst horror of war by the victorious side. Here a captain of horse was for the moment lord of life and death.

Under the apple-trees in the orchard Mr. Blood and his companions in misfortune were made fast, each to a trooper's stirrup leather. Then, at the sharp order of the cornet, the little troop started for Bridgewater.

As they set out there was the fullest confirmation of Mr. Blood's hideous assumption that to the dragoons this was a conquered enemy country. There were sounds of rending timbers, of furniture smashed and overthrown, the shouts of laughter of brutal men, to announce that this hunt for rebels was no more than a pretext for pillage and destruction. Finally, above all other sounds came the piercing screams of a woman in acutest agony.

Baynes checked in his stride, and swung round writhing, his face ashen. As a consequence he was jerked from his feet by the rope that attached him to the stirrup-leather, and he was dragged helplessly a yard or two before the trooper reined in, cursing him foully, and striking him with the flat of his sword.

It came to Mr. Blood, as he trudged forward under the laden apple-trees on that fragrant, delicious July morning that man, as he had long suspected, was the vilest work of God, and that only a fool would set himself up as a healer of a species that was best exterminated.

CAPTAIN BLOOD.
(Warren Kerrigan in the name-part of the Vitagraph Film, "Captain Blood.")

" I would have your lordship and the gentlemen of the jury
hear me on my defence, as your lordship promised that I
should be heard."   (*Page* 27.)

[*Picture from the Vitagraph Film.*

73

CHAPTER THREE.

The Lord Chief Justice.

IT was not until two months later on September 19th, if you must have the actual date —that Peter Blood was brought to trial upon a charge of high treason.

We know that he was not guilty of this, but we need not doubt that he was quite capable of it by the time he was indicted. Those two months of inhuman, unspeakable imprisonment had moved his mind to a cold and deadly hatred of King James and his representatives. It says something for his fortitude that in all the circumstances he should still have had a mind at all.

Yet, terrible as was the position of this entirely innocent man, he had cause for thankfulness on two counts. The first of these was that he should have been brought to trial at all; the second that his trial took place on the date named, and not a day earlier. In the very delay which exacerbated him lay, although he did not realise it, his only chance of avoiding the gallows.

Easily, but for the favour of fortune, he might have been one of those haled, on the morrow of the battle, more or less haphazard from the overflowing gaol at Bridgewater to be summarily hanged in the market-place by the bloodthirsty Colonel Kirke. There was about the colonel of the Tangier Regiment a deadly despatch, which might have disposed in like fashion of all those prisoners, numerous as they were, but for the vigorous intervention of Bishop Mews, which put an end to the drumhead courts-martial.

Even so, in that first week after Sedgemoor, Kirke and Feversham contrived between them to put to death over a hundred men after a trial so summary as to be no trial at all. They required human freights for the gibbets with which they were planting the countryside, and they little cared how they procured them or what innocent lives they took.

What, after all, was the life of a clod?

The executioners were kept busy with rope and chopper and cauldrons of pitch. I spare you the details of that nauseating picture. It is, after all, with the fate of Peter Blood that we are concerned rather than with that of the Monmouth rebels.

He survived to be included in one of those melancholy droves of prisoners who, chained in pairs, were marched from Bridgewater to

Taunton. Those who were too sorely wounded to march were conveyed in carts, into which they were brutally crowded, their wounds undressed and festering. Many were fortunate enough to die upon the way.

When Blood insisted upon his right to exercise his art so as to relieve some of this suffering, he was accounted importunate and threatened with a flogging. If he had one regret now it was that he had not been out with Monmouth. That, of course, was illogical; but you can hardly expect logic from a man in his position.

His chain companion on that dreadful march was the same Jeremy Pitt who had been the agent of his present misfortunes. The young shipmaster had remained his close companion after their common arrest. Hence, fortuitously, had they been chained together in the crowded prison, where they were almost suffocated by the heat and the stench during those days of July, August, and September.

Scraps of news filtered into the gaol from the outside world. Some may have been deliberately allowed to penetrate. Of these was the tale of Monmouth's execution. It created profoundest dismay amongst those men who were suffering for the duke and for the religious cause he had professed to champion.

Many refused utterly to believe it. A wild story began to circulate that a man resembling Monmouth had offered himself up in the duke's stead, and that Monmouth survived to come again in glory to deliver Zion and make war upon Babylon.

Mr. Blood heard that tale with the same indifference with which he had received the news of Monmouth's death. But one shameful thing he heard in connection with this which left him not quite so unmoved, and served to nourish the contempt he was forming for King James.

His Majesty had consented to see Monmouth. To have done so unless he intended to pardon him was a thing execrable and damnable beyond belief; for the only other object in granting that interview could be the evilly mean satisfaction of spurning the abject penitence of his unfortunate nephew.

Later they heard that Lord Grey, who after the duke —indeed, perhaps, before him —was the main leader of the rebellion, had purchased his own pardon for forty thousand pounds. Peter Blood found this of a piece with the rest. His contempt for King James burst out at last.

"Why, here's a filthy mean creature to sit on a throne. If I had known as much of him before as I know to-day, I don't doubt I should have given cause to be where I am now." And then on a sudden thought: "And where will Lord Gildoy be, do you suppose?" he asked.

Young Pitt, whom he addressed, turned towards him a face from which the ruddy tan of the sea had faded almost completely during those months of captivity. His grey eyes were round and questioning. Blood answered him.

"Sure now we've never seen his lordship since that day at Oglethorpe's. And where are the other gentry that were taken? —the real leaders of this plaguey rebellion. Grey's case explains their absence, I think. They are wealthy men that can ransom themselves. Here awaiting the gallows are none but the unfortunates who followed; those who had the honour to lead them, go free. It's a curious and instructive reversal of the usual way of these things. Faith, it's an uncertain world entirely!"

He laughed, and settled down into that spirit of scorn, wrapped in which he stepped later into the great, hall of Taunton Castle to take his trial. With him went Pitt and the yeoman Baynes. The three of them were to be tried together, and their case was to open the proceedings of that ghastly day.

The hall, even to the galleries —thronged with spectators, most of whom were ladies —was hung in scarlet; a pleasant conceit, this, of the Lord Chief Justice's, who naturally, enough preferred the colour that should reflect his own bloody mind.

At the upper end, on a raised dais, sat the lords commissioners, the five judges in their scarlet robes and heavy dark periwigs, Baron Jeffreys of Wem enthroned in the middle place.

The prisoners filed in under guard. The crier called for silence under pain of imprisonment, and as the hum of voices gradually became hushed, Mr. Blood considered with interest the twelve good men and true that composed the jury.

Neither good nor true did they look. They were scared, uneasy, and hangdog as any set of thieves caught with their hands in the pockets of their neighbours. They were twelve shaken men, each of whom stood between the sword of the Lord Chief Justice's recent bloodthirsty charge and the wall of his own conscience.

From them Mr. Blood's calm, deliberate glance passed on to

consider the lords commissioners, and particularly the presiding judge, that Lord Jeffreys' whose terrible fame had come ahead of him from Dorchester.

He beheld a tall, slight man on the young side of forty, with an oval face that was delicately beautiful. There were dark stains of suffering or sleeplessness under the low-lidded eyes, heightening their brilliance and their gentle melancholy. The face was very pale, save for the vivid colour of the full lips and the hectic flush on the rather high but inconspicuous cheekbones. It was something in those lips that marred the perfection of that countenance; a fault, elusive but undeniable, lurked there to belie the fine sensitiveness of those nostrils, the tenderness of those dark liquid eyes and the noble calm of that pale brow. The physician in Mr. Blood regarded the man with peculiar interest, knowing as he did the agonising malady from which his lordship suffered, and the amazingly irregular debauched life that he led in spite of it —perhaps because of it.

"Peter Blood, hold up your hand!" Abruptly he was called to his position by the harsh voice of the clerk of arraigns. His obedience was mechanical, and the clerk droned out the wordy indictment which pronounced Peter Blood a false traitor against the Most Illustrious and Most Excellent Prince, James the Second, by the grace of God, of England, Scotland, France, and Ireland, King, his supreme lord.

It informed him that, having no fear of God in his heart, but being moved and seduced by the instigation of the devil, he had failed in the love and true and due natural obedience towards said lord the King, and had moved to disturb the peace and tranquility of the kingdom and to stir up war and rebellion to depose his said lord the King from the title, honour and the regal name of the imperial crown —and much more of the same kind, at the end of all of which he was invited to say whether he was guilty or not guilty.

He answered more than was asked.

"It's entirely innocent I am."

A small, sharp-faced man at a table before and to the right of him bounced up. It was Mr. Pollexfen, the Judge-Advocate.

"Are you guilty or not guilty?" capped the peppery gentleman. "You must take the words."

"Words, is it?" said Peter Blood. "Oh —not guilty." And he went on, addressing himself to the bench. "On this same subject of words, may it please your lordships, I am guilty of nothing to justify any of those words I have heard used to describe me, unless it be of a want of patience at having been closely confined for two months and longer in a fetid gaol with great peril to my health and even life."

Being started, he would have added a deal more; but at this point the Lord Chief Justice interposed in a gentle, rather plaintive voice.

"Look you, sir; because we must observe the common and usual methods of trial, I must interrupt you now. You are no doubt ignorant of the forms of law?"

"Not only ignorant, my lord, but hitherto most happy in that ignorance. I could gladly have forgone this acquaintance with them."

A pale smile momentarily lighted the wistful countenance.

"I believe you. You shall be fully heard when you come to your defence. But anything you say now is altogether irregular and improper."

Enheartened by that apparent sympathy and consideration, Mr. Blood answered thereafter, as was required of him, that he would be tried by God and his country. Whereupon, having prayed to God to send him a good deliverance, the clerk called upon Andrew Baynes to hold up his hand and plead.

From Baynes, who pleaded not guilty, the clerk passed on to Pitt, who boldly owned his guilt. The Lord Chief Justice stirred at that.

"Come; that's better!" quoth he, and his four scarlet brethren nodded. "If all were as obstinate as his two fellow-rebels, there would never be an end."

After that ominous interpolation, delivered with an inhuman iciness that sent a shiver through the court, Mr. Pollexfen got to his feet. With great prolixity he stated the general case against the three men, and the particular case against Peter Blood, whose indictment was to be taken first.

The only witness called for the King was Captain Hobart. He testified briskly to the manner in which he had found and taken the three prisoners, together with Lord Gildoy. Upon the orders of his colonel he would have hanged Pitt out of hand, but was restrained by the lies of the prisoner Blood, who led him to believe that Pitt was a peer of the realm and a person of consideration.

As the captain's evidence concluded Lord Jeffreys looked across at Peter Blood.

"Will the prisoner Blood ask the witness any questions?"

"None, my lord. He has correctly related what occurred."

"I am glad to have your admission of that without any of the prevarications that are usual in your kind. And I will say this, that here prevarication would avail you little. For we always have the truth in the end. Be sure of that."

Baynes and Pitt similarly admitted the accuracy of the captain's evidence, whereupon the scarlet figure of the Lord Chief Justice heaved a sigh of relief.

"This being so, let us get on, in God's name; for we have much to do." There was now no trace of gentleness in his voice. It was brisk and rasping, and the lips through which it passed were curved in scorn. "I take it, Mr. Pollexfen, that the wicked treason of these three rogues being established —indeed, admitted by them —there is no more to be said."

Peter Blood's voice rang out crisply, on a note that almost seemed to contain laughter.

"May it please your lordship, but there's a deal more to be said."

His lordship looked at him, first in blank amazement at his audacity, then gradually with an expression of dull anger. The scarlet lips fell into unpleasant, cruel lines that transfigured the whole countenance.

"How now, rogue! Would you waste our time with idle subterfuge?"

"I would have your lordship and the gentlemen of the jury hear me on my defence, as your lordship promised that I should be heard."

"Why, so you shall, villain —so you shall." His lordship's voice was harsh as a file. He writhed as he spoke, and for an instant his features were distorted. A delicate, dead-white hand, on which the veins showed blue, brought forth a handkerchief with which he dabbed his lips and then his brow. Observing him with his physician's eye, Peter Blood judged him a prey to the pain of the disease that was destroying him. "So you shall. But after the admission made, what defence remains?"

"You shall judge, my lord."

"That is the purpose for which I sit here."

"And so shall you, gentlemen." Blood looked from judge to jury. The latter shifted uncomfortably under the confident flash of his blue eyes. Lord Jeffreys' bullying charge had whipped the spirit out of them. Had they, themselves, been prisoners accused of treason, he could not have arraigned them more ferociously.

Peter Blood stood boldly forward, erect, self-possessed, and saturnine. He was freshly-shaven, and his periwig, if out of curl, was at least carefully combed and dressed.

"Captain Hobart has testified to what he knows —that he found me at Oglethorpe's Farm on the Monday morning after the battle at Weston. But he has not told you what I did there."

Again the judge broke in:

"Why, what should you have been doing there in the company of rebels, two of whom —Lord Gildoy and your fellow there —have already admitted their guilt?"

"That is what I beg leave to tell your lordship."

"I pray you do, and in God's name be brief, man. For if I am to be troubled with the say of all you traitor dogs, I may sit here until the Spring Assizes."

"I was there, my lord, in my quality as a physician, to dress Lord Gildoy's wounds."

"What's this? Do you tell us that you are a physician?"

"A graduate of Trinity College, Dublin."

"Good God!" cried Lord Jeffreys, his voice suddenly swelling, his eyes upon the jury. "What an impudent rogue is this! You heard the witness say that he had known him in Tangiers some years, ago, and that he was then an officer in the French service. You heard the prisoner admit that the witness had spoken the truth."

"Why, so he had. Yet what I am telling you is also true, so it is. For some years I was a soldier, but before that I was a physician, and I have been one again since January last, established in Bridgewater, as I can bring a hundred witnesses to prove."

"There's not the need to waste our time with that. I will convict you out of your own rascally mouth. I will ask you only this:

How came you, who represent yourself as a physician, peacefully following your calling in the town of Bridgewater, to be with the army of the Duke of Monmouth?"

"I was never with that army. No witness has sworn to that, and I dare swear that no witness will. I never was attracted to the rebellion. I regarded the adventure as a wicked madness. I take leave to ask your lordship," (his brogue became more marked than ever) "what should I, who was born and bred a Papist, be doing in the arms of the Protestant champion?"

"A Papist thou?" The judge gloomed on him a moment. "Art

more like a snivelling, canting Jack Presbyter. I tell you, man, I can smell a Presbyterian forty miles."

"Then I'll take leave to marvel that, with so keen a nose your lordship can't smell a Papist at four paces."

There was a ripple of laughter in the galleries, instantly quelled by the fierce glare of the judge and the voice of the crier.

On trial for his life! In next week's UNION JACK you will hear the outcome. The days will seem all too long till next Thursday, when you can continue this magnificent tale. Follow Captain Blood through his breezy adventures, and he won't disappoint you. Why not tell your friends about him, too?

The BLACK EAGLE —and Captain Blood —
NEXT WEEK!

OUR next issue will be another special number. The serial, of which you have had so "moreish" a taste this week, will be continued in another and more thrilling instalment. In this it will be described how Peter Blood is sentenced to death, but escapes the noose, only to be sold into slavery in Barbadoes. There his adventures begin in earnest, and from slave to pirate chief proves to be but a short step. Captain Peter Blood has many a thrill in store for you.

And as to the Sexton Blake story, it is —
The MONTE CARLO Mystery

A typical, intriguing, well-told detective yarn this by the creator of Yvonne, Rymer, and other popular characters. The scene of it is set in the pleasure-city of the South. Throughout the yarn flits that grim figure, the Black Eagle, the man from Devil's Island.

and many original U.J. cover designs and sketches offered soon for your solution to a baffling murder mystery story to be published in an imminent issue. Details next week.

Now available in a Stillwoods Edition.../drf

TO NEW READERS.

PERHAPS you were rather doubtful when you invested your twopence in this issue of the UNION JACK. YOU saw that it contained the opening chapters of Sabatini's great story and thought you'd risk it. Well, perhaps you've read through this complete tale of Sexton Blake, too, by now. What do you think of it? We think it's good. But OUR opinion doesn't matter —we'd like to know what YOURS is. This yarn of the great detective and his lovable young assistant, Tinker, is merely one of many. We publish one —complete —every week. They're all superlative stuff; this is an average example. As you follow the future adventures of Captain Blood, you'll begin to know more about Sexton Blake as well, for, of course, you will not neglect these yarns. And wonderfully fascinating you'll find them, too. You've placed your standing order for the "U. J." —of course?

82